HANNIGAN'S HAND:

THE GHOST WOMAN TALKS!

Mulberry Books

"One of the best....one of the funniest, fuzziest books encountered!"

...CBC Radio

"A wild romp of a verse about a family's efforts to cope with the effects of a hair-shedding dog."

....London Free Press

"Uses the poetic techniques children love, rhyme and metre. The illustrations are lively, and the story is full of punch."

...Kitchener-Waterloo-Record

"Stylish, stylized, richly textured pictures capture the manic mood of the text.....attendant chaos of the subject matter appeals to young children."

..Quill & Quire

"Delightfully Daffy!"

...The Observer, Montreal

"Comical and original."

..Copley News Services, Washington, DC

"Should stand the test of repeat readings!"

...Atlantic Books Today

-JEREMY JECKLES HATES FRECKLES: (In Print)

"A great little book!"

...Crayon Animation, Montreal

"Freckled readers will relate to this light-hearted approach to a common problem.

..Canadian Materials, Canadian Library Association

"Teaches as it entertains....a lot of fun....loud message, subtly delivered.

...Books In Canada

""Delightful freckle frustration."

..The Evening Telegram

"Humorous...fascinating....well told.....deals with issues that most adults would dismiss as trivial, but which are important to children.

...The Newfoundland Herald

"Deals with the concept of specialness, and how each child should be valued for being unique and special....thank you for writing this delightful book.......

...Library Resources, NL

"Children responded very positively, demonstrated high level of interest and enthusiasm towards subject matter...found antics of Jeremy to be hilarious, and could easily identify with his dilemma....comprise the necessary elements of a Children's Literature genre-good plot, plenty of action, identifiable characters, expressive illustrations....

...Kathy Lee, BA (Ed.) BA
    French Immersion Specialist

-MALCOLM THE KLUTZ: (In Print)

"Obviously special...the result of Ryan-Lush's desire to help make the transition from picture books to novels of young readerhood...for children who are just getting into reading but not ready for the dynamics of a longer novel....avoids overwhelming her young readers with too many characters and sub-plots...funny, poignant....as an award-winning children's author, Ryan-Lush had the perfect solution...create a series of books specifically tailored to be child's first novel....

...TV Week

"Well-written as usual...this one has the same zippy energy that is so attractive in her work...

...Anne Millyard, Publisher, Annick Press, Toronto-New York

"I quite enjoyed Malcolm K. Wall. His narration gives the action energy and humour.

....Kids Can Press, Toronto

"Ryan-Lush has firmly established herself as a children's writer of high calibre....a worthy addition to the shelves of children."

...The Evening Telegram

BOOKS FOR ADULTS by Geraldine Ryan-Lush (In Print)

-Once When I Wasn't Looking (Poetry Collection)

****
****

HANNIGAN'S

HAND:

THE GHOST WOMAN TALKS!

ABOUT THE STORY:

Many years ago, a young Dan Hannigan witnessed a horrific headless spectre, and poltergeist activity which shook him to the core. A priest had to intervene, to exorcise the demon which invaded his campsite, and him, following his haplessly using a remote beach trail for some summer work. The priest told Dan he was being punished by the spirits of a tragic shipwreck which had happened there a year before. They had died before their time, and now, restlessly wandering, had claimed the trail as their own. He told him he was cursed, and, while exorcising the demon from his spirit-possessed arm, also told him *he was never to repeat what happened at the camp that terrible night, or the same curse would be upon him, and anyone else who heard the story.*

Sixty years passed. Old Dan Hannigan mellowed, and began to believe the priest's warnings were all hogwash. Until a visit from a long-ago friend and four innocent teenagers prompted the telling of the story again. *Things start happening. THE SPIRITS ARE BACK, MORE VENGEFUL THAN EVER! The ghost woman of the grate will not rest!* The four teenagers will never be the same. And Old Dan Hannigan? Is he just a crusty old codger who stepped in a ghost path many years ago, or is he now........*SOMETHING WORSE!*

HANNIGAN'S
HAND:

THE GHOST
WOMAN TALKS!

Mulberry Books
St. John's, NL
2015

ISBN 978-0-9682805-9-1

Mulberry Books
27-A Pasadena Crescent
Suite 204
St. John's, NL
Canada A1E 4S4

Table Of Contents

For my parents, R.I.P., and all the kitchen raconteurs, who gave me the genesis

CHAPTER ONE

Forbidden

"I don't see why we have to go to bed so early," muttered Shelley O'Brien, poking in her sister's makeup bag for more mysterious glam treats. " We just got here, for Pete's sake. It's not normal. And it's not *fair* either!" The twin sisters had just arrived in Aspen Falls, at the 150-year-old saltbox that had been in the O'Brien family for generations, and which was now used as a summer home. They had been relegated to the top third floor to rest, and go to bed early, after the 10-hour drive in from the city.

"What are we supposed to *do* anyway? Cable and Net have no connection here, there are only two T.V. stations, and I've already read all the books we've brought. Besides, it's hardly even dark! " With an even more disgruntled groan, she peered out at the beautiful sunset through the ancient green blind that covered the window. "This is torture. I'm crying child abuse."

Suddenly, her sister Sherry called out excitedly. "Come over here! I've found something. Look at this. " She was leaning, or lying
over, a black, grid-iron opening in the hallway, put there when the house was built, for the purpose of allowing heat to rise from the kitchen. They could look directly down through the grid openings at the metal stovepipe snaking up, up three floors from the kitchen ceiling.

"Look, you can look down at all of them and see and hear everything they're doing! Now we don't have to be bored!"

"Sweet!" Shelley's mood changed immediately. She loved excitement of any kind, and there was little of that to be had in Aspen Falls , unless you went to the Seniors' Centre and played cards. They had loved Aspen Falls as little girls, but now they grumbled about going, all to no avail. Their father hated the city, and talked non-stop about Aspen Falls all year long, counting the days until his holidays began. The girls positioned themselves prostrate over the opening, and soon it grew dark.

"I got a great idea! " whispered Shelley. "Let's leave off the light and let the moon shine in. Its more spooky that way. Wow, the guys from *Ghosthunters* would love this place. Maybe we'll hear some weird sounds, and see some shapes or something , so we can call them to investigate." She draped a sheet around her, and swaying ghostily, started moaning *"whooo-oooooooo"*........She was almost tempted to bring the Ouija board out , from under the bed, the one she had found in eccentric old Mrs. Dodd's trash back in the city, and which she had taken great pains to keep hidden ever since. Her parents would have a fit, and Sherry would be freaked out. It was all in fun, but the two girls had no way of knowing that their innocent holiday in the old house would soon turn into a nightmare, and that they would never, for the rest of their lives, want to hear the word *ghost* again!

****

Shelley had pushed back the long, carpeted, rubber-backed runner which had concealed the grid opening out in the hallway. It had been an effort. The runner was stuck like glue, having been there for maybe fifty years, and specks of mouldy, yellowed rubber were flying in the air.

"Mom will kill us." said Sherry. "We'll have to put that runner back after."

"Okay, okay." said Shelley, her sheet-encased form gliding spirit-like around the room. "We'll put it back after. But it stinks. It needs to be thrown out. What did they expect anyway, sticking us up
here with nothing to *do?* "

There were three bedrooms on each side of the long, narrow hallway, and a tiny bathroom with a clawfoot bathtub, which the girls fought over incessantly, and increasingly, as they got older. Shelley switched off the pullchain on the naked lightbulb in the ceiling, and peered down into the old kitchen.

They had been hearing stories of Old Hannigan for years now, the famous old Aspen Falls man who was a living legend; the man their father said told so many great stories when he was a kid. He was scheduled to make an appearance tonight. "Shhh! He's coming in!

They're all getting excited," Sherry reported, her nose dug in so deep in the grid it was in danger of getting scorched from the woodstove heat seeping up. The talk and laughter below went on for about an hour. Old Hannigan had not lost his touch. Suddenly, the kitchen went still. An eerie chill crept through the two girls keeping watch so high above, why they didn't know. It grew deathly quiet. You could hear a pin drop below in the creaking old kitchen.

"Yes, I remember that one. " Old Hannigan was saying. "How could I ever forget. I've been carrying him around with me for sixty years."

"Carrying what?" Shelley whispered. She could never keep quiet for long, and the limited vision of the checkered grid opening was making her frustrated. "Shhhh!" Sherry poked her . "Keep quiet! He's about to tell the story, the BIG ONE, the one Dad wouldn't let us hear because it would give us nightmares. Now we're going to hear it straight from the old man himself!"

CHAPTER TWO

The Man With No Head

The whistling of the tea kettle on the red-hot damper of the woodstove drowned out the beginning of Old Hannigan's monologue. Mrs. O'Brien liked to do all the old-fashioned things when they went in to the old saltbox: cook in the woodstove, use the whistling tea kettle simply because it whistled , and light the oil lamp, with its two- hundred- year- old reflector, in its ancient stand on the wall. The girls could hear the rattling of dishes too, as Mrs. O'Brien laid the quaint, white, drop-leaf table, swathed in a gleaming, red-checkered oilcloth, not a modern one. She had had a hard job finding that oilcloth. She eventually had to have it ordered in; but she had to have it, since it all went with the overall atmosphere of the place.

The oil lamp in its 100-year-old stand on the wall in the kitchen, and the massive, battery-operated radio on the radio shelf over the kitchen table completed the picture. Shelley wished her mother hadn't picked this particular moment to become all 60's authentic. The rattling of dishes and the whistling of the tea kettle was all getting on her nerves, and she *so* wanted to hear the beginning of Old Hannigan's most famous ghost story of all, told by the man himself, as happened to the man himself, and which they weren't supposed to hear, because it would give them nightmares.

"I'm going down." She said finally. "I want a snack anyway. This is ridiculous. We should be able to hear that story. We are not babies."

"If you go down, Old Hannigan will lose his mood and train of thought for a moment, and end up not telling it at all." Her sister theorized. "Just stay put. Give Mom time to get her Famous Tea all in order. This is a big thing for her, you know."

Shelley grunted reluctantly. Her mother was a mainlander, born and raised in Toronto. She had electricity all her life. She never roamed meadows, played tidley, swam in the ocean , or heard a ghost story in her life until she met Mr. O'Brien. Newfoundland lore and legends fascinated her, and Old Hannigan was a local she could only previously conjure up from a Poe or Dickens novel. Here she was, hearing a pure, original local speak of HIS EXPERIENCE WITH THE PARANORMAL, right here in the original old saltbox where her husband had been born and raised. Yes, it was important to her! She had the ghetto blaster, with its cassette tape recorder all set to roll, discreetly hidden in one of the cupboard doors, and planned to record for posterity every word Old Hannigan said.

The girls hovered over the grate again, straining to catch the heat from the connected stovepipes snaking up through three ceilings. The house seemed to shiver with a wierd chill all of a sudden. The sunset had turned to a grey fog all in a matter of seconds, and an aggressive wind had whipped up.

Now and then they could hear the wood crackling as their father kept the old Waterloo fed with thick junks of silvery birch from the loaded barn outside. They could hear Old Hannigan's slow, low drone as their father mentioned shipwrecks of decades ago all around Newfoundland's coast.

"Yep, you sure picked a fine spot to camp that night, Dan." He was saying to the silver-haired, spindly-legged man. "There had been a wreck there only a year before, and people were always hearing the screams and cries of the passengers who had drowned. "

"Yeah, we had heard the stories. But you know, there were always wrecks happening, and we needed that timber we had been cutting. Just wish we hadn't placed it where we placed it, that's all. " Old Hannigan's voice dropped down a decibel, low and deep, seeming to drop right into his boots. " Oh, I can remember the darkness, black as tar, but not so black that I couldn't see *him.* "

All was quiet again. Sherry looked at Shelley quizzically, but Shelley was listening intently, her intuitive blue eyes large with interest. The white sheet she had been clowning around with was still draped over her, glowing in the darkness. Who needed the Ouija board! This was even more exciting! She was betting on what the *Ghosthunter* guys would think if they were here now, with their blinking, orb-flashing monitors, and recorders grounding out guttural messages from the other side.

"We had finished up for the night." Old Hannigan was continuing. "Cut a lot that day. Great for the props for the schooners we were building ; cut that much we didn't know where to put it all. There were some old beaten paths in the woods around the beach, so we didn't see any harm in throwing the timber there."

"You sure found out differently after, didn't you." Mr. O'Brien prodded.

"You betcha. Our cabins were right by the beach. We were all ready to turn in for the night. I went down to the beach to get some air for a few minutes. It was a nice night; not a breath of wind was stirring. But what I saw as I walked along the water's edge will stay with me until the day I die."

Now no dishes rattled, or the tea kettle whistled. Nobody moved, nobody dared to breathe or sigh. Everyone was suspended, ready to jump at even the sound of their own voices as the howling wind grew angrier. Sherry moved in closer to Shelley, forgetting they had been arguing over hair combs and lip gloss all day.

"At first I thought it was one of the boys," Old Hannigan went on. "So I strode along. He seemed a long way away at first, and I was thinking that none of our men were as big and stout as this man was. He started to come closer. He was almost upon me, and I was about to say hello or something, when I realized I was just looking at bone and gristle, and blood-soaked shoulders. No head or face. He was walking towards me, a big, blood-soaked, mass of a man, AND HE DIDN'T HAVE A HEAD!"

CHAPTER THREE

Poltergeists

"Lord, you must have got some fright." Mr. O'Brien said, hooking the damper with the lifter and shoving in another junk. "What did you do then?"

Old Hannigan paused and cleared his throat. He took a long drink of the steaming second cup of tea Mrs. O'Brien had silently placed before him. The junk dropped into the fire with a loud thud. The old man stared at a square in the faded canvas as, head bent, he went on with the story:

"Well, he was coming at me, a mass of black dark moving, and there was an awful, decaying smell coming from him. I knew it wasn't human, what I saw. I mean, it was human at one

time, but not now. I almost fainted right there. I
thought I would die with fright. I was just a lad,
you must remember. I wanted to run, but I was so
weak with fright my legs wouldn't cooperate. I
somehow managed to stumble back to the cabin,
sure he was behind me all the way, sure I could
hear him stomping through the beach rocks, sure
I could smell that graveyard smell. When I got
back, they told me after, I just mumbled
something about *a man with no head* before I
passed out cold on the floor. "

Shelley and Sherry felt as if they were
mummies lying there on the grate, frozen in a
fascinated horror, wondering what Old
Hannigan would say next. Then, a massive gust of
wind seemed to be taking the roof off over their
heads, and rain was pounding in
heavy grey sheets outside their window. The
wind was driving the rain in, underneath the sill,
in little rivers that were making the old , sickly-
green blind blotched and bleak-looking, They
were used to sudden changes in weather, who
wasn't in Newfoundland, but this attack
was eerie, coming as it did on the heels of Old
Hannigan's memory digging. As it turned out,
the wind and rain and chill seemed to
parallel the next segment of the old man's
narrative.

"I came to on the cabin floor, and the whole place was shaking like an earthquake, even though it was a dead calm night. Everyone was asking what was going on, why the two cabins were shaking, and tables and chairs and things were falling over. The bunks flew off from the wall and crashed to the floor. Everyone just cowered, and huddled in corners. I was so in shock all I could do was mumble what I saw. After awhile the racket calmed down. They got me some tea and put me to bed in a sleeping bag. The next morning the foreman called to everyone. He was a stern man, but now was looking very white in the face, as if he had got a fright. He asked who had messed with the flour sack of oatmeal he had opened, to cook for breakfast. When he went to pour some out, the sack just caught fire in his hands! The oatmeal was ruined. He held up the sack for us to see. And his fingers, which were blistered from the burns. The sack was black and charred at the bottom. Everyone stared, and shook their heads. We had been too terrified to move, let alone mess with a sack of oatmeal. Then one of the young fellows, shaking and shivering, whispered to me that he also, had seen fire; a fire that had blazed out of the boulders all of a sudden, out by the cabin window. I whispered to be quiet. We didn't want the foreman to be angry at us, and send us home. We needed the money, for school in the fall. "

"The foreman said we should get down on our knees and say the *rosary.* I knew then that *he* knew that I had seen a spirit, not of this world. And that the fire in the oatmeal sack, and the fire in the rocks, and the bunks coming loose and the tables and chairs whizzing around with not a breath of wind , was all coming from that man with no head. It was while we were saying the *rosary* that I noticed my left arm and hand was swollen to three times its normal size, and was fiery red. It seemed there were insects, *things,* crawling around inside, in the skin, but I couldn't get at them. It was driving me crazy! The foreman wouldn't look me in the eye. He just said I should go home, that I had some kind of infection or blood poisoning in my arm. But I knew it was no blood poisoning. And he knew it too. It came from that -that PERSON   I saw on the beach!"

CHAPTER FOUR

Storm Cries

Suddenly, there was blackness. The blackness of a tomb. The tomb was alive, with horrible shrieks and cries of the wind as it whistled shrill along the eaves. The wind itself sounded lost, angry, in a quest for punishment, as it roared throughout the house with a desperate, haunting vengeance. The lights had gone out. Even the extra little oil lamp in the corner, Shelley's favourite, the one with the cobalt blue bowl, had flickered quickly out. The girls screamed and jumped up from the grate. Down below their father was shouting . "Electricity's gone. Stay put , girls! We're coming up. Don't move!"

The hallway was now Arctic-like cold. They could hear the window panes rattling in the merciless wind, and the hinging and grinding of the floor joints as they fought against the monstrous force. Through the lightning flashes Shelley saw black , tattered , bird-like objects winging through the air like bats. Horrified, she realized sickly they were pieces of felt blowing off the roof. *Was the roof blowing off the house?* She had never seen a storm like *this* before!

Finally , Mrs. O'Brien appeared at the top of the stairs, carrying the large, freshly-lit oil lamp from the kitchen, the same one from the stand on the wall that had flickered out for no reason.

"Are you okay, girls? My goodness, what a storm! *This* was not forecast. It only said maybe a shower tomorrow, and certainly not this wind!"

"Why did all the lights go out, even the oil lamps?" Shelley asked, shivering, huddling with Sherry over the grate. She was goosebumped all over, with the cold, and with fright, and she was not one to frighten easily. Mrs. O'Brien tried to sound cheerful. "The lamps went out for a few minutes. Your father forgot to fill them up, after all, and the wicks needed trimming. And when I tried the electric lights they were gone too. But that's just the wind , of course. It will all be back soon. What are you doing out in the hallway? And why is the mat all askew like that? What am I going to do with you girls? You pulled it back, didn't you, that old runner that's been stuck there for decades. I'll have a mess tomorrow, cleaning up all those old rubber bits. Guess it's time it was replaced." She bustled around, in the comforting arc from the oil lamp in her hand. After awhile Shelley got over her fright when the blackness descended right in the pivotal part of that horrid old story.

"We heard people down in the kitchen. We thought Taylor and Trevor were coming over." Sherry said.

"No, I'm glad they didn't now, with this weather! Some neighbours dropped in. Your Dad is bringing Mr. Hannigan home in the SUV. Come on. Come down and get a snack and get ready for bed. It's *freezing* up here!"

The girls were cramped and cold and aching. They gladly followed their mother down the stairs, seeming to jump at every shadow the oil-lamp was making on the pealing, flower-papered walls. Portraits of old ancestors lined the stairwalls, one above every step. Their penetrating eyes seemed to move with them, and their grim, austere mouths with the bushy moustaches seemed to be issuing a warning: How dare they poke their noses into the dangerous realm of a forbidden ghost story! *This is what you get,* one old dour ancestor in an ancient oval frame seemed to be saying. *You get scared half to death. Good for you. Now maybe you won't be as likely to hover over grates anymore.* "

Downstairs, there was a noisy bustle, as the neighbours got their things and prepared to hurry home. The storm was getting worse.

"Worst winds I've ever heard around here, I think." Old Hannigan was saying cheerfully. He seemed to have forgotten his story, but Sherry and Shelley hadn't. Shelley looked at him, the wiry, wizened old man still living by himself in his quaint little house up the road. It was hard to imagine he had been through such a horrific experience in his youth. But she was too cramped and tired and sleepy and scared to pursue it further in her mind. Mrs. O'Brien oven-toasted them some bread, the buttered *bread-in-the-oven*, yellow-crisped, that they liked better than actual toast; the *delicacy* their father had when he was a boy here. Their father was in a good mood in spite of the storm. In fact, he seemed to revel in it.

"Well, girls, eat up. We can manage fine without electricity. See, we've got hot tea and *bread-in-the-oven* and bricks wrapped up in flannel so you won't be cold in bed. This is how the pioneers did it. This is how I grew up. Did I ever tell you we were a rare breed, not getting electricity here until the 1960's, even though we were only two hours from St. John's? " Mr. O'Brien ate heartily of his *bread-in-the-oven* and sipped his mug of steaming tea.

Later, tucked up in the bed upstairs, their feet caressing the hot bricks and swathed in wool-crocheted eiderdowns, with the little blue oil-lamp winking friendly at them again, Shelley would have been comfortable and content had it not been for the memory of Old Hannigan's story. Whenever she closed her eyes, she could see the blood-soaked , headless figure, and smell that awful smell ,and her stomach churned. She would *never* get to sleep tonight! She wanted to bring it up to Sherry, but decided against it when she heard a loud yawn coming from her sister. "God, I'm so tired." Sherry mumbled, and after another hour of tossing and turning Shelley dropped off with her, to sleep fitfully in wild, terror-driven dreams.

CHAPTER FIVE

Ghostly Questions

Shelley woke first. She didn't know what woke her, the sunshine streaming in, or the zapping of the speedboats as they sped their way up the harbour. She poked Sherry, who was still snoring beside her. "Wake up! It's a gorgeous day." She glanced at the clock on the bureau. Twelve noon! Why did her parents let them sleep so long? She looked out the window. The high, three-storey , slanted-roof house overlooked the Bay, and the water was blue and clear as glass, broken only by the white foam that was being whipped up prettily from the speedboats. Shelley couldn't believe the change in weather from the night before. What a night! She shivered. She was going to forget all about it and enjoy the day. Taylor and Trevor should be over today. They had driven down with Uncle Max and family from Harrisville yesterday, and were staying in the dormered, old-fashioned house over the meadow.

She couldn't wait to tell them about Old Hannigan and the headless ghost. Taylor and Trevor were her cousins, and as different as chalk
and cheese. Trevor was quiet, read a lot, and liked music. He and Sherry got along well. Taylor was bold and brash and adventurous. She knew once he heard about the story of last night, he would be all over it, especially the part

about the insects in Old Dan Hannigan's hand. Downstairs, delicious smells were wafting up through the grate and into the girls' nostrils. Sherry yawned and sat up. "Ummmm. What's that smell? I'm starved!"

"Figured that would wake you more than anything." Shelley said, unzipping Sherry's makeup bag and piling its contents on the bureau top. Sherry always liked her stomach. They ran down the three flights still in their pajamas, and found their mother humming with the old Newfoundland waltzes coming from the radio Mr. O'Brien had set up out in the yard. She was presiding over a huge teapot covered in a blue-flowered tea cosy, a pot of fragrant coffee, and the oil-cloth-draped table laden with a breakfast from heaven. The girls crowed in delight as one by one, they grabbed a blueberry pancake off a platter, devouring it, forgetting their manners in their ecstasy. They bantered over which way they liked them. "I love them with butter and syrup." Sherry gushed, her cheeks like a chipmunk as she chewed.
"Butter only for me", Shelley said. "Lots of it , and melting in rivers."
There was bacon and sausage, whole wheat toast, porridge, fresh fruit, jam, molasses and cream. Shelley looked it all over.

"Gosh, Mom. I know you enjoy cooking, but you know, it's your vacation too, and you don't need to be *Aunt-Jemima-In-The-Kitchen* every morning while we are here. The pancakes and *bread-in-the-oven* are treats enough!" She stuffed her face with another pancake, blueberry juice staining her chin, and melted butter dripping from her mouth.

"Here, messy, use a napkin," Sherry said, handing her a bunch. Mrs. O'Brien smiled indulgently, and poured herself more tea from the teapot. "I wouldn't miss this for the world. And yes, I will be making breakfast every morning. Everything tastes so good, out here in this air." The girls ate lustily until taking a break, Shelley's face took on a serious look. "Some change in the weather this morning. Gosh, Mom, that was a wierd thing that happened to the lamps last night. They just went OUT, all of a sudden!"

Her mother looked a bit tense. "Y-Yes, well, that happens sometimes when there is not enough kerosene."

"But I thought Dad filled them up yesterday."

"No, he forgot." Shelley looked at her mother. She was hiding something. She herself had seen her father filling up the lamps yesterday, trimming the wicks and cleaning the globes with newspaper, the old-fashioned way, whistling, happy as he always was as soon as they arrived in Aspen Falls.

"It was nice seeing Mr. Hannigan. When is he coming down again?"

Mrs. O'Brien paused before she spoke. "Oh, I guess he'll be by in a few days. He is getting along, you know, and his mind is not what it used to be." Shelley shot a look at Sherry. There didn't seem to be anything wrong with Old Hannigan's mind last night. He was spry and fit as a fiddle. Her mother knew they had been listening at the grate last night, and was trying to spare them fear, and possible nightmares, by stating it was the old man's mind; and that there was no essence to the horrible story, or part of the story they had heard. Her mother had got a scare, Shelley thought. She usually thrived on ghost stories, and kept up the excitement of them long after they were told. But this one was different. Her mother didn't want to talk about it. "It's so beautiful out today. Not too hot. What are you girls planning to do?"

Shelley sat, her elbows on the table, looking through the kitchen window with the wide sill, on which rested pots of geraniums and other plants her mother had brought. She loved the wide-silled windows of this age-old house, like shelves, where you could place any kind of collectible. Scenic, hand-painted rocks kept company with whimsical homemade ornaments, and candid family photos. A cheery cafe valance topped the window. Her mother had expressed a wish, being big-city bred, of putting blinds on the windows, but her father had laughed it off. "No need for blinds around here." he said. "When I was growing up no one even locked their doors at night. That's how trustworthy everyone was."

"Well, I don't know if I would go *that* far." Her mother said wryly.

Shelley sat gazing at the view. She could see why her father had it in his blood, and still believed in the innocence of the place. Rolling green meadows sloped up as far as she could see and beyond, dotted here and there with stately maples in full foliage, and apple trees in full blossom. Their white petals were floating lazily towards the ground, in the windless, still day, and she could smell their perfume drifting in through the open window, as well as the fragrance from the fresh lilacs in the vase on the table. Violet-colored, lilac trees were her favourite, nodding in their simple splendour just outside. Truly, this place was paradise. It was hard to believe she had been so scared last night. How could *ghosts* or anything unpleasant live or lurk in such *beautiful* surroundings?

CHAPTER SIX

The Woman In The Grate

There was a bang on the door, startling Shelley out of her nature-worshipping reverie. She jumped, and when the bang reverted to a series of rapid, staccato-like *bang-bang-bang-bang-bang-bang-BANG!* she gave a whoop of joy. It had to be Taylor and Trevor! It was Taylor's signature knock. She rushed to the storm door, and swung it open to find a grinning, chubby-faced, suntanned Taylor, beaming at her from the weathered, wooden doorstep, all urbane and cool in his khaki shorts and runners.

"Hall-oo There Cuz! What's up?" He was chewing on a wad of bubble gum as usual, and his black eyes were flashing merry devilment. His curly black hair danced with zestfulness. Shelley looked forward to Taylor and Trevor's annual visits all year long. It was the only thing worth going to Aspen Falls for. She had hordes of cousins from both sides, but they were her favourites. Sometimes, she thought she had a crush on Taylor , as Sherry had on Trevor, but that was ridiculous. They were cousins! But if they weren't....well.....hmmm... she let that nice gem play in her brain for a second as Mrs. O'Brien emerged all smiles from the backyard, after hearing Taylor 's deepening, pleasant voice.

"Why, hello Taylor! My, you've grown so tall and handsome in a year! Where's your Mom? I'm dying to see her."

"Hello, Aunt Laura." Taylor's newly broadening shoulders went automatically back with the praise, and he poised himself to stand straighter. "You're looking lovely as always, and your flowers are absolutely stunning. I'm always telling the florists in Harrisville about my Aunt Laura's gardening jewels. Showed them some digital pics, too. They're quite impressed." Taylor flashed another of his disarming smiles, and Shelley's Mom flushed pink with the praise, until she remembered what a charmer he was. She chuckled. "You're one smooth operator, Taylor O'Brien. The girls will have to watch it with you." She left to go over the meadow to see Taylor's Mom. Taylor paced the old kitchen canvas excitedly, wanting to know all the latest news. Sherry came into the kitchen from upstairs, all showered and changed into a new, fresh pink shorts set, her long, blonde hair tucked back with a smartly matching scrunchie.

"Hi! Where's Trevor?"

"Oh, he'll be along. You look quite fetching, Cuz. " Taylor liked to use sophisticated terms like *fetching*, which he had learned from his older brother who was in the Armed Forces. "You two are getting to look so much alike I can almost no longer tell you apart. What's new? What's up? Anything exciting?" Taylor kept up the pacing, and Shelley found herself telling all about the strange happenings of the night before, but she would not repeat Old Hannigan's story, the one that started it all. She was afraid to repeat it, why she couldn't figure out. "Mr. Hannigan was down and told ghost stories, and the lights went out." She finished.

"Wow! Whoopee Wow! That's so cool!" Taylor was in his element. "I always wanted to meet that old codger. Just didn't get a chance yet."

"He's not an old codger." Sherry defended. "He's actually just a nice old man. We've known him since we were small kids. And he was around when Dad was a kid. He's ancient."

"Oh, don't be so sentimental. He's an old salty codger with loads of cool ghost stories in his head. I just know it. Come on, let's go for a walk up the beach."

"In a minute. I have to change." Shelley eyed Sherry's fresh new shorts set again. She climbed the stairs to the little bedroom. After she dressed, she went in the bathroom . She hurriedly pushed her hair up in a ponytail, and splashed fresh cold water on her face. She brushed her teeth, and spying Sherry's makeup bag again, she giggled. None of that for her. She just wanted to enjoy the day. She smoothed sunblock lotion on her face while she moved to the music coming from below. The door to the bathroom was open, and she could see the exposed grate, into which black, heat-diffused, checkered holes they had looked down into last night. She could hear Old Hannigan's voice, and see the ghastly, headless creature in her mind. She shivered. She felt cold all of a sudden. The whole room felt cold, numbing, like when she opened the massive deep freeze in her parents' basement back in the city, to get steaks for supper. The arctic chill was back. She was a lone, freezing entity against the hot, steaming, day outside. She felt sure someone was standing right next to her, almost brushing against her shoulder, almost breathing down her neck. Something propelled her to walk to the hallway, and push back the runner again, which her mother had swept off that morning, until she found time to buy the new one and replace it. Then her breath caught in her throat. She felt strangled. A woman's face stared out at her, her mouth moving, trying to form words. *There was a woman in the grate!*

The woman was real, with long blonde hair, matted and wet. As was her form which drenched clothes clung to her in a sodden, sea-stuck glue. Her eyes were dilated in a hopeless terror as they gazed up at Shelley. Shelley clapped her hands over her mouth, her stomach doing a nosedive, as she jumped with shock. She pushed back the runner again. She waited, and took deep breaths. She couldn't tell the others about this. She must be imagining it. She had to be! In a few moments she lifted the runner again. Nothing was there, except the quivering clumps of grey dust which clung to the edges of the iron squares. She *had* been imagining it! Shakily she ran downstairs.

"Let's go." She told the others. She felt so cold, the sun didn't seem hot enough to bring warmth and life back into her chilled bones.

Taylor was grinning and pacing impatiently. "Cool. You're ready. Let's get this show on the road!" He was carrying his shiny new metal detector and bragged about it all the way. After awhile turning up bottle caps and useless pieces of scrap with the detector , they had reached the dunes. They could see Old Hannigan's house from there, perched prettily at the top of a slanted green meadow.

"Let's go up and see the old codger." Taylor blurted. "Maybe we'll get another story out of him."

Old Hannigan was mowing the grass when the kids went up the long, tree-lined lane to his house. He was using a sycthe, a primitive, long, hooked blade, not a modern grass-cutter, and he was using only his right arm and hand, even though the sycthe required the use of both arms moving in careful, rhythmic motions to work properly. He was wearing overalls, a short-sleeved, checkered shirt, and suspenders. His left arm was dangling limply by his side. Shelley stopped in her tracks. Old Hannigan's arm and hand was swollen to three times its normal size, and the skin was fiery red, just like he had described it last night after he had seen the grotesque headless man so many years ago!

CHAPTER SEVEN

A Change In Mr. Hannigan

"Mr. Hannigan, what happened to your arm?" Shelley tried to keep the alarm out of her voice. The old man looked tired and frail all of a sudden, all in the space of one night. His hearty spirit had vanished.

"Oh, it came on all of a sudden. Bit of arthritis I guess. " He tried to smile a toothless grin and put down the sycthe. "Come on in the house. I could do with a break. " He wiped the sweat from his forehead with an already drenched red handkerchief. As he slowly lifted his left arm to wipe his face, Shelley gasped in horror. Black ooze, with a sickening mixture of what looked like crawly worms was coming out of his hand and arm! She looked again. Riddling up his shoulder were ladders of red, oozing blisters and puffy , rising mounds!

He was walking with a wobble, and didn't seem aware that his arm was in such a state. Shelley swallowed hard and looked at the others. She must have imagined the worms thing. This could not be real! She had been awake half the night last night, flopping among the bedcovers in hideous, tortured dreams, and then that woman in the grate! Her mind was playing tricks on her. She motioned to the others who were busy talking.

"Come on. Let's give Mr. Hannigan a hand. He's tired, after all the mowing." The three kids helped the old man to the kitchen, and made him lie down on the old-fashioned, leather-covered settle.
"Mr. Hannigan, your arm is really sore." said Shelley, trying to keep her voice calm and not daring to look at him. "Maybe we should send for the doctor."

"No! No doctor. Doctor can't cure what is wrong. Couldn't cure it sixty years ago. " He sighed. "I knew I shouldn't have done it."

"Done what, Mr. Hannigan?"

"Told that story last night. But, luckily, I only told part of it." Forcefully ignoring his remarks, Shelley got some fresh spring water from the

dipper out in the porch, and put on the kettle for a
cup of tea. "You have a bad sunburn, Mr. Hannigan. It's blistering. I'll bandage it for you."

   Old Hannigan stared at Shelley with a panicked, feverish glint in his eyes. He hastily covered his bad arm with his other hand. "No! Don't touch it. Don't touch it. It's not a sunburn. I know what it is. But it's not for you kids to know." He sank back against the pillow and closed his eyes. "Let sleeping ghosts lie. Let them be. Let them be."

   "What's that, Mr. Hannigan?" But the old man was already dozing, even in sleep his good arm around his bad one protectively.

   "Have a nap, Mr. Hannigan. We'll do some chores for you." Maybe her mother was right, Shelley was thinking , and his mind was really not what it was. Taylor did some chores outside while the girls did what they could to make the inside comfortable. Mr. Hannigan was used to living alone, and as he took a nap Shelley and Sherry roamed around, peeking in rooms. After awhile Sherry grew impatient.

"Let's get out of here." She said. "This place is starting to give me the creeps, it's so close and suffocating all of a sudden."

"Remember how we used to love to come here when we were little?" Shelley said, trying to forget Mr. Hannigan's wormy arm. "Remember how we used to love to sit at the circular bench around the woodstove and drink tea from Mr. Hannigan's pretty flowered dishes? The little dish set that belonged to his little girl."

"You mean the one who died?"

"Yes. He gave me her cradle. Remember?" Sherry stared at her sister. "No, not really. Come on. Let's get out of here. This place is giving me the creeps."

CHAPTER EIGHT

The Barn Poltergeist

Shelley knew Sherry was anxious to see if Trevor was around. They were running down the lane when they heard what sounded like the jingling of horse bells, and a low, eerie growl coming from the darkness of the barn. "What's that??" Shelley's eyes were wide.

"I don't know. But I'm not sticking around to find out." They both took off, Shelley lingering and looking back towards the barn. Old Hannigan's old barn had fascinated her as a child, when she had found a little mahogany baby's cradle one day. Mr. Hannigan said it had belonged to his little girl who had died a long time ago, and that he would like for her to have it. Her friends were spooked, saying the cradle could be haunted by the ghost of the little girl who had died, but Shelley loved it. She kept it in her room and rocked her dolls in it until she grew too big for dolls. She smiled to herself and kept looking back as they made their way down the long lane lined with buttercups and daisies . The air was sweet from the wild red rosebushes that grew so abundant between the picket fences, freshened by the tangy sea air. The bells were tinkling even louder. They could hear whinnying horse sounds, and loud , playful clomping and trotting like horse hooves.

"Let's go in the barn!" Shelley exclaimed, once again caught up in the beauty of the day. What could possibly happen on such a peaceful, beautiful summer's day in Aspen Falls? She knew wierd things were happening, but the sunlight helped her forget, at least for a time. But she could not forget the woman in the grate, and the bathroom like an icehouse. She pulled on Sherry's arm. "Come on. Let's go up to the barn. I'd like to see if that's Lisa. I'd love to see Lisa!" She remembered her fondness for Old Hannigan's pet pony. But Sherry's eyes were wide, blue pools of fear and irritation.

"Are you crazy? You can go. Alone. I'm not going near that old place. It always gave me the creeps, and it's worse today."

"Oh, come on. I'll let you wear my new earrings this evening. They're silver, and they dangle. They'll go with your blue denim jeans."

"Uhh...okay. Gee whiz, you always know where to strike hardest."

Shelley laughed, knowing full well her sister's vanity, and budding love of fashion. Sherry wanted to look perfect at all times, and they were both secretly hoping Trevor had brought a male friend or two with him.
"But the minute I say *let's get out of here* we scoot. Agreed?"

"Agreed."

Together they walked up to the barn, which, like Mr. Hannigan's other outbuildings, still looked the same as it did forty years ago. They went inside, and tried to adjust their eyes to the gloomy , clammy-feeling darkness. The one, lime-scaled, cobwebbed window was littered in old, rust-encrusted farm implements, and what little light that was filtering in was shadowy and dappled, blocking the girls' view. Suddenly, the wide, grey, ramshackle door that had lain open on one hinge, its corner embedded into the soft ground, flew up and banged shut with a loud bang, of its own accord!

CHAPTER NINE

Terror In The Barn

A piercing scream came from the twins at once. They looked around. There was no way out! There was no friendly Lisa the pony coming to greet them, but something, a *creature,* with cloven feet and winkers, and standing about twelve feet high! Shelley 's breath came in gasps. Her voice seemed gone suddenly. Oh, why did they have to come up here on such a beautiful day, and find Mr. Hannigan all wierded out like Ichabod Crane or somebody, his house so close and spooky, and now *this, this monster!* Why did they have to be in the middle of all the evil that was happening after Mr. Hannigan's visit last night?? That woman in the grate, and now *this!!*

"It's the devil!" Cried Sherry, bumping into Shelley in her fright. They were in total blackness. "Run! " She yelled hysterically. "Run! Run! He's after us!"

"Run where?" Shelley yelled back hoarsely. "The door, it won't open!" They had stumbled their way to the door, fumbling desperately for the rough-hewn slab of plywood wrenched into its socket, which acted as the door's makeshift latch. They lifted it and pulled, with all their might, to push open the door, but the creaky old artifice wouldn't budge. "Kick! Push!" Shelley screamed. Behind her she could feel the creature's breath.

They rattled and pushed and kicked the door, the darkness and putrid odour overpowering them so much they almost fainted. The creature was clomping towards them. They could hear him: closer, closer, a low, rumbly, terrible growl coming from deep inside his cavernous, evil gut. He was growling, and stinking, from ancient, filthy, graveyard clothes, and any second now he would have them in his grasp! Then Shelley lost her footing. She toppled over into the insect-infested earth of the barn. Beetles and spiders were crawling up her feet! She screamed again and kicked them off, pulling herself up and finding the strength to give the door one last heave.

"Lift!" She yelled at Sherry. "Help me lift up the door!" The corner of the shabby, lime-patched door was embedded in a soft sod square that Mr. Hannigan had thrown there only yesterday. Shelley positioned both arms under the primitive board backing, and using every last ounce of strength they lifted the door about four inches, out of its stuck, trapping hole. It was enough for them to frantically squeeze into the tiny space, and to glorious freedom outside! They ran, tumbling one on top of the other, as Shelley tripped on a sawed-off tree stump!

She lay there, paralysed in terror, looking up at a horrific
figure, the sun blocking out the features. All she could see were old, tattered, musty-smelling clothes, and a towering creature with nothing only shoulders! Wet, slimey, bright-red blood was creasing slowly down them!

"Oh My God!" She gasped, her breath coming in strangles. "It's *Him! The Man With No Head!"* She was starting to faint. She was really going this time. The ground was spinning under her. Mr. Hannigan's house only a few feet away was blurry and toppling; she felt like Dorothy in the Wizard of Oz when the tornado happened. Then, she heard a laugh, a deep, guttural, gleeful laugh....*Wooooo......Waaaaa.......* as *The Thing* reached out to claw at her, lying helpless on the ground!

CHAPTER TEN

Punishing Spirits

The Thing bent closer. He was big, and broad-shouldered, and black and menacing. Flesh and gristle seemed to be where a head should be. *Bloody* flesh, gristle, and bone. But he was exhaling, close to her ear. A bloody,headless monster breathing in her ear! She could feel his foul breath, decaying, hissing. She was starting to faint again.

Then her jaw dropped, as she saw grinning white teeth and dark, curly hair, peeking through the holes in the cloak! She gasped, in relief, anger, and embarrassment. It was Taylor! In old horse gear, moth-eaten, moth-balled clothes, and stalking on four-foot-high wooden stilts! The stilts were what did it, what made him seem like a gigantic, menacing phantom, from her vantage point on the ground. They raised his height about four feet. The girls had never seen stilts before.

Shelley got up, her face greased in dust and grime and sweat. As much as she liked Taylor, right now she wanted to kill him.

"You-you scared us half to death! How dare you play a trick like that! We-we thought you were the MAN WITH NO HEAD!" She was trembling violently from head to foot, in fear and anger.

"The Man With No Head!!!??" Taylor guffawed loudly. "*What* are you talking about? I found this old shroud, is all, and some old horse gear, and thought it would be fun to dress up. And all kinds of half-open gallon cans of red and grey and black paint and glue and stuff. I drew some skull bones and stuff, and poured some paint. And those stilts! They're so cool! I did a good job, didn't I? WHOOOOOOO...."
Taylor's black eyes glinted evil again, and he grinned wide in vampirish delight.

"How dare you make the door fly up like that and trap us!" Sherry accused, shivering with anger. "We almost killed ourselves trying to get out!" Taylor's face looked sheepish through the layers of paint he had smeared on. He hadn't meant to do them any real harm.

"I didn't touch the door. I hid, up in the loft and waited for you to come in. I jingled the horse bells to entice you, since I knew how much you loved Lisa." Taylor attempted another slippery grin. Shelley and Sherry looked at each other. "You mean you had nothing to do with the door flying closed on its own? It just *flew up.* There was no wind, and it was stuck like glue in a hole." Shelley was getting cold shivers again. How much more was going to happen after Old Hannigan's story last night! Taylor laughed, in an intriguingly impish way.

"A door flying open on its own on a calm day....hmmmm...this is *interesting.* A big, heavy old door that was embedded a foot down into caked , dry mud. A door that had been embedded like that for years, maybe decades. And no wind, you say. Jeez, Maybe there are *ghosts* about! For that matter, maybe there are *poltergeists* about! Wow, I would love to see a *real, honest-to-goodness ghost!* And I would give all my Dracula comics to see a *real, honest-to-goodness-poltergeist!* " He smiled, in a dreamy way.

"You wouldn't think it so funny if you had heard what we heard last night."

"What was it? What did you hear?" Taylor leaned closer, coaxing.

"Did Old Hannigan tell another story of someone seeing a white horse and fainting and having the priest called? Or another pirate who buried treasure in the rocks and murdered a cabin boy to guard it with his ghost? *Whhooooo....awwww.......*love it!!! " Taylor was smacking his plasticine-covered lips with glee. Sherry was getting angrier by the second. Her pink suit was wrinkled, and covered in grass stains. Her lovely, new pink shorts suit that she had worn to impress Trevor. She would never get the stains out. Grass stains were the worst. She was hot and disheveled, and her hair, perfectly styled that morning, now hung in sweat-drenched wisps about her face.

"Well, we're not going to tell you, are we, Shelley." She fumed. "What you need is a good scare all your own. Then you'll be laughing on the other side of your face." She noticed a rip in her chic, sleeveless blouse which made her even angrier. "Taylor, I hope you get so scared......." But Taylor was throwing off his disguise, and clomping around on the stilts. He was clearly having a ball. "Me? I don't get scared of *nothing.*"

"Anything." Corrected Sherry. Mad as she was, she was forever the grammar freak.

"Whatever. Around here in those places, away from the city, and with no electricity all those years ago, people saw their own shadow and were frightened to death. That's where all the ghost stories came from. I love listening to them, but I don't believe in them. It's the highlight of the year for me, coming here every summer and hearing those ghost stories.

" So tell me about The Man With No Head." He shot another of what he thought was a disarming grin the girls' way and kept clomping on the stilts. The sharp, triangular bottoms dug ruthlessly into the ground, making deep ruts.

"You're going to ruin Mr. Hannigan's meadow," said Sherry. "He was telling Dad he had just finished the new sodding, and how nice the grass is. Mr. Hannigan loves his meadows."

"Aw, to hell with the old codger." Taylor said defiantly. "So obsessed with his stupid grass he can't let a kid have a bit of fun." He clomped and clomped until he had his fill of the fascinating stilts and threw them on the ground carelessly.

"So tell me about The Man With No Head." He kept on, fishing melted chocolate bars from his pockets and offering some to them as a peace offering. But the girls wouldn't touch the inedible, dribbly candy, not if they were starving to death. They were still too angry at the evil deception that had ruined their clothes and their day, with the fright. "You'll find out soon enough." Said Sherry, eyeing her ruined shorts again, and not knowing how soon that prediction would come true.

CHAPTER ELEVEN

The Water Ghost Woman

Mr. O'Brien wasn't long keeping up his tradition of the annual bonfire on the beach , which he organized with the kids every summer as a treat. The beach, or seashore, ran the whole length of Aspen Falls, as did the ocean, which it bordered. The section of the beach in front of the O'Brien place was accessed by going down the meadow, across the gravel road, and down a grassy lane. Several old fish flakes and stageheads dotted the beach, and were now more artistic than used, when people from the city came in to take photos.

Mr. O'Brien started directing the very next evening. "Now kids, get busy. If you want a bonfire, you better start gathering the supplies. Take the wheelbarrow and see what you can gather up. I'll supply the splits and kindling. " The mound on the beach that night at dusk was something to behold. Driftwood and old cardboard crates kept company with broken furniture and chairs. The pile, tindered with dried branches and twigs, promised to be the most successful bonfire ever.

At ten o'clock, the fire was raging high, sending rivers of sparks into the starry sky. The kids whooped with delight as they kept the fire fed, throwing on anything they could find. They would get as close to the fire as they dared; then, their faces hot and smokey, they would jump away again. Taylor was in his element as usual, dancing around:

"Dance, Dance, wherever you may be, I am the Lord Of The Dance, said she, and I'll lead you on, wherever you may be, and I'll lead you on in the

dance, said she....... " He pranced around, like a beguiling Celtic Fiddler of old.

 "Say, Uncle Bob, how about we all tell some ghost stories?" Mr. O'Brien was strangely quiet for a minute. "I think we've had enough of ghost stories for awhile." He said, as he put wieners on sticks made from twigs. "Here, start burning some wieners. That will keep you occupied for awhile." Taylor's disappointment soon turned to delight.

"Ohh..smoked weenies roasted on a stick...." He crouched by the fire and started turning twigs with wieners stuck in them over and over.

 "Weenies." scoffed Sherry. "You're such a city slicker." She was still waiting for Trevor to show up with his guitar, and still smarting over her ruined pink suit. The kids kept feeding the bonfire, and Mrs. O'Brien and some neighbours soon arrived. Trevor finally showed up, his guitar on his back, and quietly started playing. They all broke out singing. They were all arguing over who was the more popular, Justin Bieber or Bryan Adams, as Shelley idly admired the moon-sparkled water's edge. Then her breath caught in her throat. There was a woman walking up from the water's edge, straight out of the bottomless depths of the sea!

CHAPTER TWELVE

Evil Presence On The Beach

She was a young woman, dripping wet, with long ,blonde hair, and carrying a baby. She was dressed in a flowered dress, with a wrap over her shoulders, and was moving with a fluid grace. Her long clothes seemed to wave across the moonlight. Her blonde hair was stringy and matted , her drenched clothes clung to her willowy frame. She looked directly at Shelley, her expression troubled and sad, her arms outstretched. Shelley's blood seemed to drain from her body. It was the woman in the grate!

Shelley stood baffled, stunned, shocked, and suddenly chilled right to the bone. The air all around her was sub-zero, although the fire licked upwards in hot flames close by. Again she felt like she was in the deep freeze. She was shivering uncontrollably, and her teeth chattered and rattled against each other in cold and fear. Panic seized her. A ghost! A REAL GHOST this time! It had to be real. She had seen it twice! Then she gave herself a shake. She couldn't get all hysterical and tell the rest she had seen a ghost!

The lovely bonfire would be spoiled, and it was just so beautiful and romantic here on the beach. Wonder who *she* is though, thought Shelley. It was weird, what was happening to her. She was almost paralysed with fear, but she still wondered who this ghost was, and why she was trying to get her attention.

Shelly gave herself another mental shake. She was imagining it, there was no ghost. Maybe she is just part of an actors' troupe , the Performing Arts Group, or artists and painters retreat people who visited the settlement every summer. Pretty late to have a baby out, though, Shelley considered. And she walked right out of the depths of the sea! Shelley tried to control the chattering of her teeth as she asked the others a question.

"Who is the lady with the baby?" They all looked, but could see nothing.

"What lady?" asked Taylor, stuffing bits of black, burned wieners in his mouth with relish, and guzzling down his can of Pepsi. "The one just up there, walking on the beach." But when she looked again, the lady was gone. Where did she go??? She had seen her.

She was there one minute, the next she was gone. There was nowhere for her to go. She had to be there! The flakes and stages were a way up from the water's edge. She would not have had time to reach them and become hidden in their shadows before Shelley had looked for the second time. Shelley felt a coldness creep over her again, and a wierd feeling in the pit of her stomach. She ran up the beach, fear gripping her, but the need for her own peace of mind outweighing that fear. She had seen a lady, a lady with a baby, in a long dress and wrap, who had looked directly at her, beseechingly. She had seen the same lady in the grate, back in the house. She knew now she wasn't imagining it. Where was she? Where had she gone? She saw nothing, heard nothing, only the gentle lapping of the water, and the laughter and singing from the group by the bonfire echoing down. She walked back. Maybe I imagined it, she thought again. Maybe she was not over the scare yesterday from being trapped in the barn, and Taylor's pranks. But she knew she didn't imagine it. She was too REAL.

CHAPTER THIRTEEN

The Captain Without A Face

"Are the Performing Arts Group here this year?" Shelley asked Aunt Miriam, who would know.

"No, there's nothing going on of this nature here this year." Aunt Miriam answered pleasantly. "Couldn't get the funding. You know how they all depend on government grants, and I guess the new government is cutting back this year." Aunt Miriam was scolding Meaghan, who was getting too close to the fire and had scorched her dress. "Going to do some acting , are you Shelley? You would be good at that. Aunt Miriam smiled at her.

Shelley forced a grin, glad Aunt Miriam couldn't see her pale face, white and cold as stone. She was so cold she felt like a block of ice, and it seemed there was an unknown presence there, on the beach; a hovering, evil presence that had come uninvited, and was meaning to stay; a presence that feeded on revenge. Shelley

moistened her dry lips with her tongue. No Arts this year. So who was
the woman? She had to be a ghost! Her hands felt clammy, and ice cold at the same time. She forced herself to forget about it, she had to, and joined in the riotous singing of *Coming 'Round The Mountain*, and other camping songs, until the group finally made for home as the fire burned down. Sherry and Trevor kept singing and playing. Their melodious young voices rang out pure and harmonious in the still, clear night.

"You kids come on home now." Mr. O'Brien told them. "It's almost 1
  A.M."

"Oh, come on Dad." Sherry coaxed. "We are having such a nice time. Just a little while longer....please? Trevor's teaching me some new chords....."

"Well, I don't know. The fire......"

"I'll take care of the fire, Uncle Bob." Trevor spoke up. Mr. O'Brien looked at Trevor. He liked Trevor. So quiet and responsible. He liked him better than that other rapscallion, Taylor, who was always making mischief, always asking what the latest excitement was. "Besides, Dad, you can look up the beach and see us from your upstairs window." said Sherry, plucking on Trevor's guitar strings happily.

"Well....okay. But no later than two. Is that clear? And I want that fire completely out."

"Thanks Dad." Sherry excitedly broke into another song. Before very long Shelley, Sherry, Taylor and Trevor were all that were left on the beach. The minute Mr. O'Brien's back was turned, Taylor started throwing more driftwood on the fire. "Hey, Dad said......" Sherry started, but only lamely, since she was already into still another new song.
"We can't let it die yet. What fun is that?" Taylor smirked, defiant as always.

"Let's walk up the beach a bit." He said, after awhile, bored with the low-key guitar playing. "I'm stuffed with wieners, and I need to see what other excitement this ghostly night holds. WHOO....AAAA! It's only just begun.....the bewitching hour. WHOO...AAA." He pranced along, kicking rocks with the toes of his sneakers.

"But we can't leave the fire..." Shelley said, still trying to get the image of the woman out of her mind. "We'll bank it first." Trevor said. He went to the water's edge and filled up buckets of water to douse the flames. Second time back, he looked at Taylor with a strange look on his face.

"You go down now." He said.

"But I've done all the work tonight. " Taylor said. The two brothers were not known to argue. Shelley thought of the woman she had seen, and the scent and feel of something evil and angry, and sad. Had Trevor felt it too? Had he seen the woman?

"Here, give me the bucket," said Taylor. "Geez, why is everyone acting so skittery all of a sudden?" He ran down to the water's edge, swinging the bucket brazenly. They looked after him. The moon was full, the water calm and peaceful. He came back with a full bucket of water.

"See, there's nothing or no one down by the water. Except maybe a few ghosts...." He heehawed loudly.

The fire doused well with water, and sand over the ashes, the four of them left the smokey heap and walked up the beach. They walked past fish flakes and stageheads, their worn, dark, skeletal foundations striking black against the lavender sky , taking on an eerie, luminous beauty all their own. Shelley and Taylor ran under, and in and out of some of them, chasing each other.

They had walked the mile as far as the part of the beach which bordered Old Hannigan's place. They could see his house, nestled in its tree-lined nook at the top of the lane, silhouetted against the moonlit sky , like a pictureesque Hallowe'en ad. It was different from most places where old, lonely people lived. It was pretty, not spooky at all. Old Hannigan's house was an artistic sight day or night, and photographed and captured by many tourists and artists who travelled to Aspen Falls.

   Shelley couldn't help wondering how the old man was doing. She shivered when she thought of him saying the sunburn on his arm was not a sunburn , and the memory of the worms crawling out of his arm made her nauseous, not to mention the insects, and leeches digging their way into the flesh, sucking the blood and gradually the life out of kindly old Mr. Hannigan. It was like a horror movie. *Something is going on here. The awful storm the night we came, the woman in the grate, the woman on the beach, the barn door flying closed and trapping us, Mr. Hannigan's demonic arm, the evil presence that's all around, waiting....watching....*

Suddenly, a loud scream from Taylor pierced the stillness!

"Run! " He shouted. "Run! Run!" The twins were shocked. Taylor of all people, to be terrified! Brazen, defiant, fearless Taylor. Shelley normally would have been glad that he got his own back, after what he had done to them yesterday, but he was so in terror! They all ran with him, gasping for breath.

"Taylor , what was it?? What did you see??" The other three asked in
chorus.

"Run! Run! Run for your lives!!!" Taylor's black eyes were wide and bulging , shiny orbs of panic. This was no joke he was playing. "It was something... a man....he was not real.....I thought he was real but he wasn't......he was dressed real cool in a captains's coat with shiny brass buttons, and a fancy captain's cap....but....but....he came out from behind one of the pillars and....and....I went over to him to say hello....to shake his hand....and....and .....Oh I can't think of it......."

"*What? What??*

"He-he looked normal at first, but then....then his face got real gaunt and ugly, and his eyes were just sockets....the sockets were full of blood and and....oh God!..........my hand went right through him! Come on! Let's get the hell out of here!"

CHAPTER FOURTEEN

The Spirits' Revenge

They ran past the flakes and stages and banked fire. As they got closer to the banked fire from the bonfire, they stopped still, staring in terror and shock. Grouped around the banked fire which they had doused so thorougly, were about a hundred people, men and women , children clutching toys, water dripping from their soaked, old-fashioned clothes; arms outstretched towards the now roaring fire which the boys had banked and put out!

The girls screamed. Taylor and Trevor grabbed them, and tried to pass through the ghost people, who looked so real, staring at them out of bewildered, desperate, and pleading eyes. There was anger too, in their empty gaze. Shelley could feel their anger ,piercing through to her extra-intuitive mind; anger at being so ruthlessly disembodied from their watery resting place;

anger that their wandering, 60-year-quest still had not given them peace.

Through the ripples of the calm water's edge, they could see more people parading up the pathway, from the depths of their sea-scooped graves, carrying sodden, broken carpetbags, and tattered remnants of a life cut short. They were screaming, high-pitched, terrified, desperate screams, while wierd laughter emanated from the ghosts by the fire. Behind them there was an ancient ship, a battered and wave-lashed schooner of decades ago, its stern open and gaping a huge hole, where it had plunged into unseen rocks, in a long- ago realm of Old Dan Hannigan's youth, tossing men, women and children screaming futilely into the midnight black, treacherous and unforgiving sea.

As Shelley and Sherry and the boys tried to pass the people, they felt themselves being pulled in by a wind like a cyclone. Rocks flew up as the wind got stronger, driftwood whizzed all across the beach, a million pebbles were zapping them in their eyes, face, hands, feet. Suddenly , Shelley was lifted high into the air, being carried towards the ghosts by the fire!

"Help! Pull me back! Pull me back! " She screamed. Her face in the ghostly firelight was white and waxen. She looked already dead, like a corpse. Suddenly Trevor started yelling "O'Brien Shelley! O'Brien Shelley!" Shelley was immediatly dropped down with a plop, on the gravel, safe from the wind. "What the...." Taylor started to ask, but there was no time. They had to make their escape.

"How did you do that? What did you yell out?" Taylor asked Trevor, trembling, his voice a whisper and his eyes rolling with fear.

"I said her name backwards. I read that somewhere, in a book about evil fairies. I just took a chance on it working. " Taylor looked at his brother in new appreciation, though still in shock at all that was happening. There was no telling what went on in a quiet guy's mind. And Trevor had been reading a lot of wierd ghost stuff lately.

"We have to get out of here! We can't let them get us. Hurry!" yelled Trevor again. There was an urgency there the others had never heard before. Taylor felt that Trevor knew things that were not of this world. And he felt the hair rising on his scalp with fear.

The four kids somehow made their way out of the wind , dragging and pulling each other. They tried to run   past the shadowy ghost people, who were lost in a limbo, who couldn't cross over to the other side, after Old Hannigan had disturbed them that awful night. They kept stumbling, tripping, falling. Trevor's 's guitar was slapping on his back, and Taylor, who could never leave his junk food, was weighed down with his backpack loaded with Pepsi cans.

Trevor tried to drag him, but suddenly he couldn't feel Taylor's 's sleeve. There was nothing. Taylor was gone! He looked back, and his heart seemed to leap from his body. Taylor was in the wind, lifted high above the ground, his backpack dangling pitifully from his shoulders. He was floating, suspended, weightless, like in a space capsule. They could see him mouth "Help! Help!" The spirits had him in their clutches. He would never get away now.

Oh, my God! Taylor's gone!" Shelley screamed, her voice a squeak with the shock of her own capture.

"Taylor's gone! He's...he's up in the air!" They looked back as they ran, the use seeming to go out of their legs with fear. Taylor had been drawn into the wind! All the ghosts were looking at him, gleeful, laughing. He was disappearing, up, into the now black and desolate sky, waving his arms wildly. Then they couldn't see his arms. Soon they couldn't see him at all! He was getting further and further away! So far he seemed like a floating ball of mist.

"Come get me! Come get me!" They could hear a tiny voice, like a windup doll, far off in the reaches of the murky clouds.

Shelley was sobbing. Taylor was gone forever. Bad, bold, kooky Taylor, who was afraid of nothing, and who she so often wanted to kill, and scream with laughter with, at the same time. Her best friend. She didn't like to think of a Taylor with a voice and a mind like a windup doll.
"We have to get out of here!" Sherry was screaming hysterically. "They're trying to steal me! They're pulling on my hair!" She was frantically tearing at her long hair, battling uselessly the clawing, hateful hands that wanted to torture, possess. But Trevor didn't hear her. He was already leaping up the beach towards Old Hannigan's boathouse.

"We have to get him back!" He yelled. "But they'll take us too!" Sherry cried. But Trevor kept running. He had to get Taylor back!

"He's not there! I can't see him!" He kept running towards the stages now. "Taylor! Taylor! Where are you? " No answer. his brother was gone. "Taylor, Taylor, where are you? Answer me! I'm taking you back! Don't be afraid! " There was a throbbing lump in his throat. He had lost his brother. The ghosts had won. "Of course you can't see him!" Shelley was crying. "He's not even human anymore. "

Suddenly, Trevor saw a movement in the door of the boathouse. A slinking movement that caught the corner of his eye. He dared to hope. Maybe it was a cat, but maybe not. He ran to the movement. There was Taylor, curled up in a ball, his arms hugging his knees! His face was pinched, the colour of parchment. He was still, huddled, terrified. "Thank goodness you're safe!" Trevor yelled, fighting back a stubborn tear.

"How did you get here? You-you were gone! We-we couldn't see you anymore. Who....what....changed you back?" But Taylor only stared at him out of glazed, uncomprehending eyes.

"Come on! We have to get back!" But Taylor wouldn't move. He wasn't able to move. *He's in shock* Trevor thought, and pulled him up, his backpack still hanging straggly down his tattered back. He ran down the beach towards the girls, towards the ghosts again, bravely plunging into their groping, grasping depths, moving through their transparent forms, any second feeling they had them in their orb again, never to be released; a slow, horrific struggle with the zombie-like Taylor, who seemed like a person in rigor mortis. Finally they had broken free!

They all dragged each other painfully until they were finally in the lane of the O'Brien home. There they fell on the ground, their sneakers full of beach rocks, their feet cut and bleeding, their faces expressing the absolute horror of what they had been through. Taylor's eyes were boggled, and his mouth hung agape. He spoke staccato-like, like a traumatized C3PO.

"They ...were... ghosts. They .....tried... to ....keep....... me. They ....wanted ...me." He didn't know where he was supposed to BE anymore. He didn't know who he WAS anymore. Taylor O'Brien was gone forever. Sherry was so in shock she tried to pretend none of it was real. She could deal with it better that way.

"Do you think we were just overtired and excited by the party, and scared by Mr. Hannigan's story that night?" She asked desperately. Taylor's rapid change shocked her. The old Taylor was gone, she knew never to return. "Maybe they were locals trying to scare us." Trevor said. "That spot where we had the bonfire is a favorite by local kids, even grown-ups. They think they own it, even though it's public property. Nobody owns a beach! But they don't like city people and tourists taking their favorite spots, so figured they would give us a good scare. And remember, a lot of locals are affiliated with the acting groups sprouting up around here."

Shelley tried to stop her trembling while Trevor talked. Trevor, sensible Trevor, loyal, logical, and level-headed. As terrified and traumatized as he may be, and he read a lot and KNEW things, he was still making a conscious effort to be rational, see it all in perspective. But she didn't believe his theory for a second. She knew what she saw, what they had been through. They were real all right, *real spirits, and somehow horribly connected with the story from Old Hannigan, that story of that shipwreck so long ago.* Old Hannigan knew. He knew he should not have opened up the past.

CHAPTER FIFTEEN

Shock And A Pact

"We have to make a pact." said Sherry, after they had all sat awhile, drinking more Pepsis from the knapsack, trying to control their fear and their thoughts. "We must not tell our parents about this. "

After the boys had gone across the meadow to the dark, dormered house they were staying in, Trevor guiding his changeling brother, the twins lingered, shaking like leaves, outside the door. The beauty of the night, the sky, and the effusive scent of roses and lilacs , more pungent and fragrant from the sea air, were all cold comfort now.

"What are we going to do? asked Sherry again, her voice quivering. "How are we going to keep this from them? I'm so scared I can't talk straight. You know they will notice."   The two girls huddled together, secretly glad they had each other to help them through.

"We have to act as normal as possible." Shelley answered. "Maybe, like Trevor said, it was people trying to scare us. Remember all the stories Dad used to tell us of all the pranks when he was a kid here? Those old ways never really went away, and old jealousies and resentments still exist here."

"Maybe." Sherry agreed, simply to make herself feel better. "But what about the ship?" she shivered. "And-and that awful wind? Taylor was stolen by that wind! We almost lost him! And-and the wind that lifted you up? And all those *people,* those *ghosts,* coming out of the water! And that old ship. *Where did it come from?* My God, Shelley, it was awful. I can't stop shaking. I think I'm going crazy." There was a catch in Shelley's voice when she answered.

"Well, we lost Taylor anyway. He will never be the same. He's just a vegetable now. " Then some part of her logical brain wanted to see a rational reason, but only for a second, and then it was gone.
"Well, it could be the actors. Maybe they had a wind machine. Like in the Hollywood movies." She gave a nervous giggle, but her voice came out cracked and shrill-sounding.

"What?? You can't be serious! A wind machine! I don't think the actors around here would be that imaginative, and those things have to be awfully expensive. Where would they even *find* one. Even if they did get arts grants, there would be no money for something like that!!" Sherry was dabbing blood from her cut big toe with a soggy tissue. *I must be in shock,* she thought, *or I wouldn't be talking so sensible about wind machines or even talking.* Shelley still felt like she had a frog in her throat, a cracked, shrill-sounding, terrified frog.

"Forget it for now." She croaked. " We must try. We will go in and go on to bed and say nothing. If we do they'll either send us to summer camp .....or keep us in at night here. And that would drive me REALLY mad." Mrs. O'Brien's voice suddenly came as she opened the storm door to find her daughters huddled together on the steps.

"Girls! Come on in! What's happened to you? You are all a mess! We were just going to look for you. It's past two-thirty!"

"Coming Mom." They rushed by her meekly and ran upstairs, before she noticed the blood on their socks from their cut feet and their bruised faces from the flying beach rocks, not to mention their smokey, torn, and tattered clothes. In their turn they went to the little bathroom, and hands shaking, prepared for bed. This time they didn't argue over space. But as Shelley started to brush her teeth, her stomach heaved, and she found herself vomiting up the smoked wieners and ginger ale she had enjoyed so much. She was violently ill from the memory of what she had seen, and exhausted, she crawled in beside Sherry, hoping for deep sleep and forgetfulness.

CHAPTER SIXTEEN

Hannigan's Hand

When the girls came down to the kitchen the next morning they were surprised to see Old Hannigan at the table, sipping tea, his arm in a sling. He was dipping his toast in his tea, and slurping on it, seeming to enjoy the comfort and company of the O'Briens. Shelley thought it strange to see him there, so early in the day; he visited sometimes but not that often, and never in the daytime. Old Hannigan always liked to visit a few favorite neighbours at night, for cards and gossip and stories when he could be coaxed to tell them, after he had his chores done for the day. He looked thoughtful and troubled and was unusually quiet.

"Hi Mr. Hannigan. Your sunburn is not any better?"

"Nah." Old Hannigan slapped his stricken arm in irritation. "I've never known a confounded sunburn to give me so much trouble before."

"Did you go to the doctor?"

"Yes, I was forced to finally. He slathered it in ointment and told me to stay in. Said it was the worst sunburn he had ever seen. And he wanted to know what those dead insects were that had eaten into my arm. He said he had never seen that species before, in all his forty years of practice. I knew where they came from, but I wasn't going to tell *him.* Old Hannigan sighed. "I wanted to tell him there was no sense in bandaging the arm; the insects were coming back, bigger and blacker."

The girls shot each other a horrified glance. Old Hannigan had aged ten years. Tufts of his hair, escaping below his fisherman's cap, were now snow white, and as he slurped his tea and toast, his large eyes were poppy and darting, in nervous agitation.

"Middle of summer and I can't go at my gardening." He slapped his arm again, at the hidden, coiling, snaking evil that lurked within. "Did you kids stay up all night with the bonfire?"

He asked, giving a wary glance out of the corner of his eye as he broke another
piece of toast in several pieces and soaked it in his tea mug for a second.

"No, we came home about 2 A.M." said Shelley, feeling herself going all cold again.

"That's funny. I looked out the window around four and the fire was raging. I was starting to get worried. Biggest bonfire I ever saw. I was surprised your Dad would let you make one that big, and have you stay out all night like that. And who were the people around the fire? What a gang!
I never saw them around here before. Are they friends of yours?"

   Shelley felt her knees go weak. She glanced at Sherry, who had turned a deathly pale.

"We came home at two, Mr. Hannigan. We doused the fire."

   "So you don't know the people who were there, the people in long dresses and torn old suits and carrying baggage? I could hear
screaming too, and an awful racket, crying, yelling. I'm sure people could hear it for miles...but when I got up this morning they were

all gone. I don't know what to make of it..." Mr. Hannigan shook his head.

Shelley answered carefully. She didn't want to alarm Mr. Hannigan. She used all the control she could muster to keep the fear out of her own voice as she answered.

"We didn't see anybody different, Mr. Hannigan. And we doused the fire. We even threw sand over it. But-but it could be anybody. Maybe the theatre group are starting up around here again, and they could have relit the fire, maybe practising for a play
or something."

"Hmmph. Don't think so. That lot couldn't get funding this year. None of that acting foolishness this year. And it's a good thing too.
Keeps me up all night with their antics and the mess they make. Bill at
the post office told me, and he knows all the news about that lot, and everything else that goes on around here."

Sherry was rattling dishes and stuffing bread on a rack to be oven-toasted . It took longer, and she didn't really want it, but she had to do something, buy time, trying to block out the horrifying fact that those parade of dripping water ghosts on the beach last night had been seen by Mr. Hannigan too!

"Well, maybe it's the Parkinsons. They always have a load of visitors in every summer. Maybe they were just fooling around."

"Well, they must have had a job getting that ship in from St. John's then," said Mr. Hannigan.

"What ship?" Shelley's voice was barely a whisper.

"The ship that was out there, in the landwash, the old rusty rotten schooner, with the hole in the stern. " Sherry dropped the rack of toasted bread on the floor. She tried to pick it up but burned her fingers and the smell of burnt bread was now permeating the air. Shelley was pouring more tea from the teapot into Mr. Hannigan's mug , with chilled, violently shaking hands.

"I'm -I'm sure there is an explanation Mr. Hannigan. Here, drink this, and have another blueberry muffin. And after you can go out and sit with Dad under the maple. It's nice and cool there."

"Humph." Mr. Hannigan rose from the table slowly, waving away the tea with his good arm. He seemed to have aged another ten years from the day before.

"Dang this arm." he said. "The use seems to have gone right out of it now. Its the bad one too. I knew I should never have brought up that story. Good thing I didn't finish it though. No. good thing I didn't finish it." Old Hannigan kept mumbling to himself as he limped out the door to the backyard. "Let sleeping ghosts lie. That's what I always say. Don't get in their way. Let them be."

CHAPTER SEVENTEEN

The Revelation

Mrs. O'Brien was worried. The girls had been acting strange lately, detached, jumpy and pale. Sherry jumped almost ten feet when she had asked her where she had put the basket of clothes from the clothesline, and Shelley wasn't saying much, and looking tense. What was going on with those two? They were at an age when erratic behaviour was the norm, but their whole personality and demeanour seemed to have changed in almost a day.

"Okay. What is it? What's up with you two? "
They were all at the supper table. Sherry's hair
was uncombed and askew, so unlike her tidy
daughter that their mother was alarmed. And
Shelley was withdrawn and unusally obedient,
doing things mechanically as if she were part of
another world. They *were* part of another world,
a world of a woman in a grate, a beseeching
ghost woman on the beach with a baby, an ugly
faceless phantom by the stage, vengeful,
murderous spirits coming out of the sea, being
taken prisoners of a death-trap wind, and a huge
bonfire that became relit after being completely
doused with seawater and burned all night long,
surrounded by out-of-body creatures screaming,
and sloshing up the beach from a ghost ship.

Not to mention Old Hannigan's diseased arm,
which was slowly getting worse. And worst of all,
that ..that..*wind* that had wanted Taylor and
Shelley so badly it almost didn't bring them back!
Shelley surprised her mother by speaking first.
Her words came out in a tumble.

"It all happened since Mr. Hannigan's visit the
other night."

"What? What happened?"

The girls told everything, this time holding nothing back. It was such a relief to release the horror of it all. Mrs. O'Brien went pale, but struggled to compose herself.

"Oh, for goodness sake girls, you mustn't believe such things! Your imagination is running away with you. You two have had almost no sleep since before we got here, and you've been reading too many books that are not fit to read. I found some in your room before we came here. And horror stuff on the T.V. and internet. I should have been more vigilant, should have caught them in time..... Mrs. O'Brien was blaming herself for her daughters' state.

"It wasn't the books, Mom. Or the internet. This was real. Taylor and Trevor saw it all too. Taylor was pulled into the *wind.* And Mr. Hannigan. He *knows.* " Shelley's voice went quiet at that.

Suddenly, there was a loud scraping from the old kitchen canvas as Mr. O'Brien pulled back his chair. He got up from the table without finishing his favourite mud trout which he had caught himself that day.

"Now, you two. I want to hear no more of this. It's crazy, insane. What you thought you saw on the beach was no more than some locals down the shore. You know that crowd down in the cove. They were always a little different, even when I was a kid here, and they're game for anything, and would DO anything for a ruckus if they could get away with it. They always got a charge out of tormenting visitors here. And that Taylor, egging you on! It's okay for him to get a good fright, it may stop his wild antics for awhile. Now forget about it all and go help your mother paper that room. A little work is what you both need, to ground that wild imagination of yours."

He spoke to them both at once, as if they were one being, not two. He often did that, since they were twins. The stern, reality lecture seemed to help though. The girls helped their mother as she fed wet cut sheets of wallpaper through the trough and pressed them into place on the walls of their bedroom. They liked the wallpaper; it seemed to soothe their frayed nerves, and finally they both fell into the first good sleep they had had since they arrived in Aspen Falls.

CHAPTER EIGHTEEN

The Wall People

Three nights later, Shelley was between awake and dreaming when she felt blowing on her eyelids. There was someone blowing on her eyelids! She sat up in bed, her heart beating fast. Sherry was fast asleep. Then the bedroom door flew open, and did she imagine it, or did the rocking chair in the corner start rocking! I am really losing it, she thought. I have to get a grip. The wick in her little blue oil-lamp was turned down low, but she picked up a book she had hidden under her pillow and tried to read, with shaking hands. Suddenly she heard whisperings in the wall, and there were banging sounds coming from behind the headboard. The banging sounds were so loud that her mattress started to shake .The empty rocking chair started rocking again, in steady, rhythmic motions, and she thought she could hear an old woman's humming, then a plaintive, wailing moan coming from it.

She felt panic rising in her again. Stay cool. You have to stay cool. You have to use your head she told herself. There has to be an explanation for all this. But there was no bedroom on the other side of that wall, and nowhere for those sounds to be coming from.

But they persisted, the moanings, the whisperings, the low wails and singing. Maybe Mom and Dad got some neighbours in she thought, and they are helping with the new partition to the extension at the far end of the house. But at this hour?

There seemed to be a number of people in the wall. She wished Sherry would awaken, but she slept on. Sherry always could sleep like a log. *I can't stand this. I have to see what's going on."* Shelley thought. Slowly, shakily, she crept out through the hallway, the creaking of her every step on the ancient floor joints making her jump with fright. The hallway was lit by another oil-lamp on a stand in one corner, and a modern, electric, scented night light was plugged in by the bathroom door. She stopped by her parents door, and could hear her father's low snore. Her parents' room was quiet, no one was visiting.

Bravely holding her breath, she attempted to creep down the stairs to the kitchen. Suddenly she was overcome with that feeling of *presence* again! *It was like how she had felt on the beach, when she had seen that woman, of someone else being there on the steps, something evil that was hounding her every step!* Halfway down, she ran breathlessly back upstairs, across the creaking hallway and into bed, huddling under the covers, stone cold once more .

CHAPTER NINETEEN

Mantra Of Disturbed Spirits

But in bed, the whisperings got worse. Much worse. And louder.
He should not have done it. He should not have blocked the path. Over and over the voices repeated the same mantra. *He should not have done it. He should not have blocked the beaten path.* Desperate now, Shelley finally poked Sherry. "Wake up! Did you hear that?"

"Hear what?"

"The whisperings in the wall."

"Whisperings in the wall? Are you crazy? Is there any way of getting sleep around here?" Sherry yawned irritably and turned groggily over on her belly.

"Not while there's ghosts. Listen. You have to hear this. Put your ear to the wall." Sherry drowsily lifted her head, still with her eyes closed, and put her ear to the wall. She came wide awake in seconds, and went deathly white.

"Oh my God, there's people in the wall! What are they saying? This is so wierd! We have to wake Mom and Dad! I'm not sleeping here tonight!"

"Listen." Shelley kept at it, although petrified. She turned bottom up a glass tumbler that had been lying on the nightstand, and put it against the wall. Then she put her ear to the glass tumbler. The whisperings came out crystal clear. *He should not have blocked the path. He should not have blocked the beaten path.* Her eyes widened in sudden, frightened clarity.

"It's all to do with Mr. Hannigan's story. Don't you see?"

Sherry leaped out of bed, now fully awake. She flinched as her bare feet touched the cold linoleum. She glared at her sister. "No, I don't see, and I don't care! Are you starting to *enjoy* this or something? I'm getting out of here! Now! "She rushed out and banged on her parents' door.

"Mom! Dad! Wake up! Wake up!" Sherry was almost banging the door down in her fright. Mr. O'Brien pulled open the door, his eyes still half shut.

"What is it? What's happened? Are you all right?" He was tying his robe and looking anxiously out of sleep-slitted eyes at the pale faces
and terrified eyes of his two daughters. "Has someone broken in??? Laura, come here!"

"There's voices, Dad, in the wall, and-and awful strange sounds. The rocking chair rocked and the door flew open, and someone-someone was blowing on my eyes!"

CHAPTER TWENTY

Old Hannigan Finishes The Story

Mr. O'Brien stared in disbelief at his daughter. This was too much. Was his happy, sensible Shelley going crazy or something? She certainly wasn't acting right since they had arrived in Aspen Falls. Was she hallucinating? Was she...no he couldn't think that....he wouldn't even *go there*.....was she on *drugs?*

"This is getting too crazy." he mumbled , running his fingers through his hair. "Tell you what. We will switch rooms. Your mother and I will sleep in your room, and you girls in ours. Now hop to it, so we can all get some sleep. We'll see about these stupid VOICES."

The next morning Mr. O'Brien was unusually quiet, his nose buried in the Aspen Falls community newspaper he rarely read because he found it too boring. He didn't finish his breakfast, and strolled outside, looking worried. Mrs. O'Brien wasn't looking as fresh as she normally did, and kept up a steady stream of chores for all to do.

Help with the new wallpaper going up the stairs. Help with the laundry. Help get the barbecue set up out by the fence to cook steaks for supper. She and the girls were exhausted by the time Shelley heard her father ask her mother a strange question. He kept his head down and wouldn't look her in the eye. They had heard the voices, Shelley thought. I just know it!

"What do you think of you and I paying a visit to Dan tonight?' Shelley heard her father ask her mother. "He maybe could use some company." Their mother put the last dish away in the dish rack and went upstairs to get ready. "Well, as long as he doesn't tell any ghost stories. I've had enough of those," she called down from the third step of the stairs.

At nine o'clock that night, the weather changed abruptly again, and
the rain and wind was whipping up in gale force gusts. Shelley thought of the eerie storm the night Old Hannigan told part of the story of The Man With No Head. Was it starting up again? Mr. O'Brien was instructing the girls.

" Now you girls, stay inside while we're gone. Don't move, do you hear me? I've got electric lights on all over the house, and the DVD player is all set up. You can stay in the living room, eat snacks, and watch a movie while we are gone. We should be back around eleven."

"Yes, Dad." said Shelley. "Yes, Dad." echoed Sherry. The girls gave their parents time to get up the road and settled away in Mr. Hannigan's house before they were spurred into action.

"Come on!" Shelley said, grabbing coats off hooks. "We have to face the music. We have to get to the bottom of this! We have to hear the rest of that story!"

"They'll kill us." said Sherry, nervously zipping up her rain slicker. "We promised to stay here!"

"I don't care." said Shelley defiantly. "Whatever they do to us it can't be worse than what we've already been through."

"Don't you see why they're going up there? Dad wants answers, and they're going to find out the rest of that story, the part Mr. Hannigan said he "didn't finish."

"What story?"

"Don't you remember it? The one Mr. Hannigan started to tell about the Man With No Head, the night we arrived." Sherry looked strange at her sister again. Shelley seemed to be really into this. She had been terrified that night also. But she had been having a nice time since with her electric roller set and sifting through the brochures for the Sears outlet up the road. Sherry wanted new clothes, new makeup, and meeting new boys, and all Shelley wanted to talk about was *ghosts!*

"I'd rather stay here than go out in that rain."
Sherry grumbled. "We have Cheese Crunchits
and Cokes, and I did want to try out my new
eyebrow shaper."

"Okay, Miss Lady Gaga. Stay here. Play with
your makeup. Put on your new eyebrows. But
I'm going. Stay here and let that old woman who
was rocking in the rocking chair and all those
people who are in the wall get you. Boo!"

Shelley made a face and ran for the door. The
porch door slammed shut as she tied up her
hood. A shriek came from Sherry, tumbling out
from the kitchen. "Wait! I'm coming! I'm
coming!"

"Thought you would, Scaredy-Cat!" Shelley
linked her arm in her sister's companionably, and
they started out towards the road.
They walked up the road towards Old Hannigan's
house, heads bent, battling the gusting wind and
driving rain. It seemed forever, and Sherry
grumbled all the way, but at last they could see
their father's SUV parked up in the lane. The
lights shone cozily and tauntingly through the
windows down at them, at the bottom of the rain-
soaked lane. How they longed to go inside, out of

the cold and wet, but their parents would freak out at their disobedience.

"We have a job to do." said Shelley. "You can stay here and help me do it, or you can go inside where it's warm. It's your choice."

"I'll stay, " said Sherry, and stopped her grumbling. Shelley signaled silently and they crept stealthily under the kitchen window, which was open partially, held up an inch by an old rotten stick stuck under it. Mr. Hannigan never ever closed his windows, not even in storms. The air from a storm was always better than any he ever breathed, he always said. The girls strained their ears to hear the bits of conversation that floated out over the wind.

Old Hannigan's voice came clear, now tired and old. "It was so long ago. I was just a lad, like I said. But I remember *everything, everything about that night, and what happened after.* I kept it inside, the secret, for sixty years. I kept my pact with that old priest. Until the other night, the night of the storm and wind. The worst storm I had seen in my lifetime, since the night of the creature, the thing with no head. It all started to happen then, after I told the beginning of the story."

Old Hannigan paused. The wind and rain kept squalling, and through the narrow opening of the window with the stick in it, the girls could see the smokey globe around the struggling wick on the oil lamp on the table, struggling as it tried vainly to stay lit inside the globe which Old Hannigan had neglected to clean since he had run out of newspapers, and his hand was bad. He still liked to live in the old way, without electric lights.

He continued, his voice becoming gravelly. "The morning after I saw the spirit, The Man With No Head, I was in shock. The cabins had nearly burst apart, tables and chairs were tumbling everywhere, dishes were crashing, bunks flew off from the walls, and worst of all, my hand and arm just kept getting worse, swollen and red, with a black, spider-like trail running right up through it. The foreman sent me home. He said I should go to see the doctor, but he knew no doctor could cure what I had. I knew it too, but I went anyway. I went to the doctor.

He gave me medicine, but nothing worked, and the hospital was too far away. I went to see the priest, up on the hill, up in his dark, gloomy, freezing house. It was a big house, a lot of big, empty rooms. I was afraid of it, and afraid of the priest too, but my hand kept getting red and inflamed, and the black, spider-like thing seemed alive as it wriggled up and down inside my arm, inside the blood vessels. I was going crazy, with pain and fear. The priest put me in one of those big, freezing, empty rooms. It was dark, but he made it darker. He told the house servant to leave the room. I was there, alone, with this formidable, fearsome man in long, black robes, and holding a wooden cross and sharp implement like a knife wielded above me. Then he closed the heavy drapes and towered over me, as I lay shivering on the iron bed. There was only a candle to light the blackness that was everywhere."

He looked at my arm and hand. He asked what I had been doing at the camp. I told him about our work, the timber, and about seeing The Man With No Head, and the cabins going to pieces. He held my arm in his black-cloth hand.

'It's a bad one.' he said. 'you have a bad, bad, curse. ' I started to shake, there on the bed. I had something EVIL, a CURSE, in my arm, my body! I was SPIRIT-POSSESSED! DEVIL-POSSESSED! THE DEVIL WAS IN MY BODY, AND I WOULD BECOME THE DEVIL! I started to cry, and scream: "GET IT OUT! OH, PLEASE GET IT OUT! GET IT OUT!"

The girls could hear Old Hannigan's rising and panicked voice through the window as he relived the horror all over again.

"Take it easy, Mr. Hannigan." Mrs. O'Brien consoled. "Here, have a glass of water." There was another pause as Old Hannigan drank thirstily from the water, his parched throat relieved by the soothing cold liquid, and ready to speak again.

"He told me , the priest did, that I got in their way, the spirits, the ghosts from the wreck, by blocking their way around. They were wandering spirits you see, they couldn't rest, they had died before their time, they had to keep moving, searching, until someone put them to rest. It was their territory, their realm, there in the grassy pathways. I blocked their way, by ordering all those grassy pathways to be loaded down with timber , the timber we had cut. The dead became restless, anxious; they wanted to punish.

Then he punctured my arm, while he moved the cross around, with the thing that looked like a knife, and lanced the curse out. He lanced the curse right out of my arm. Oh, it was hideous, awful. It shot up out of my arm, right across the room, and landed on the ceiling; it was black, wriggly, like a snake. The priest reached up and slid it down from the ceiling. He looked at it in his hand for a long time. Then he reached in a dark cupboard for some cloth wrappings. He dropped the evil thing into the wrappings, and lifted the damper from the stove. It disappeared into the flames.

'Oh that's a bad one.' he said. ' A bad , bad curse. Those spirits wanted you punished. You should never have gone near that place. All those mariners, those people from the shipwreck who drowned.....'   My arm was a gaping wound. THINGS were coming out of it.....THINGS like ....like....tiny bones and twigs and crawly worms...and big, black insects...." Old Hannigan's voice started to rise.

"Now Dan, take it easy," Mr. O'Brien said. "What you had was not punishment from an evil spirit. It was an infection you picked up. Father Mallory was an old Irish priest, full of superstition. He frightened the wits out of a lot of people around here."

"Yes, I think you're right; at least I thought I was over it, until I told it the other night, and then the swelling happened with my arm again. "

Shelley wondered why he didn't mention the worms and insects crawling out the other day. Old Hannigan's voice started to rise again as he continued in a strained, worried tone: "And something else. After he cleaned up my arm and bandaged it, the priest said if I repeated the story ever again in my life the same curse would be upon me, and *upon anyone else who heard the story.* But over the years I ceased believing that part, until the other night."

"It's all hogwash, Dan. There is no such thing as ghosts. If we let ourselves believe, the mind plays tricks on us, is all." *Tiny bones and twigs and crawly worms.* Shelley gasped. Those were REAL worms and insects she had seen crawling out of Mr. Hannigan's arm the day Taylor had scared them. So the curse was repeating itself! Mr. Hannigan was doomed. Maybe they were all doomed. She just knew that now.

"Those --those *people* ...." Shelley's teeth were chattering again from the cold wind and fear. "Those...those *people* coming out of the water the other night. They-they-were the ghosts of that shipwreck all
those years ago...." It all made sense now. Horrified, she looked down and from where they were crouched by the window they could

see the beach and the exact spot where the bonfire had been.

It didn't look peaceful now. The water was gushing in angry waves over the beach, from the rain. But what if all of a sudden the bonfire started to burn again, and those ghosts came again out of the water, clutching greedily, grabbing ,sucking them into their clawing grasp, into their WIND. They were around, she could feel it, there was heavy breathing in her ear, and she felt something touch her arm.

"Run!" She screamed at Sherry. "They're here again. They must have heard Mr. Hannigan talking......." But it was only Taylor who had touched her arm. The new, strange, Taylor who had become a different person overnight.

"Yes, it is best if we go now, " he whispered spookily.

Shelley felt he was as weird and unhinged as the ghosts on the beach. The three of them ran down Mr. Hannigan's lane and back down the road in the wind and rain, Taylor walking slower, dazed-like, hardly noticing. At the house at last, the girls kicked their wet boots off in the porch.

"We have to get upstairs as fast as we can.'
Sherry said. "Mom and Dad can't know we were
out!"

CHAPTER TWENTY-ONE

Sheer Terror

Breathless, Shelley ran first up the stairs.
Suddenly , Sherry heard a loud scream. She
rushed up the stairs. Shelley was white and
shaking. She was sitting on the fourth step up.
She was pointing at one
of the old ancestor portraits, the one in the
ancient oval frame. "What is it? What did you
see?" Sherry asked.

"The picture." Shelley 's voice came out
ragged, in a whisper. "Someone is in the picture. "
she gasped. "It's that lady, that lady on the beach,
the one that came up from the water's edge
carrying a baby. The woman in the grate. She
was trying to say something....."

Sherry looked. The picture was the same as
when they had left, the whiskered old man

staring out solemnly, from his beady, 150-year-old eyes. "Are you sure? The picture looks the same." She noticed her sister's open mouth and large, staring, terrified eyes, filled with a kind of horrified fascination.

Shelley just kept staring. "It was her. The woman. She was trying to say something, tell me something. Oh my God Sherry she looked so desperate, so pleading! She was holding out her arms toward me....."

Then Sherry screamed. And screamed. And screamed. There were *people* in all the ancestor pictures! They were moving, liquid, shadowy. The beach people, all wet, reaching out, skeletal, real men fully dressed but drenching wet; young, pretty women's faces turning suddenly to ugly old bony hags. Shelley and Sherry clutched each other, screaming hysterically. Blindly they ran for dear life down the stairs, and out the door, their stockinged feet becoming once more cut and bloody as they rushed up the road towards Old Hannigan's house. They banged on the old storm door, and Old Hannigan limped out to answer it, looking not at all surprised by the state of the girls, or their fear.

"WE HAVE TO LEAVE THAT HOUSE! WE HAVE TO LEAVE THAT HOUSE! Shelley screamed. "WE HAVE TO LEAVE THAT HOUSE NOW! IT'S HAUNTED! ALL THE PEOPLE FROM THAT SHIPWRECK SIXTY YEARS AGO ARE IN IT!

Old Hannigan nodded, in a new , eerily calm understanding. "Yes, I think it best if you should leave it." he said. "I never should have brought up that story. You will never know peace in that house now."

CHAPTER TWENTY-TWO

The Bathroom Haunting

Mr. O'Brien wasn't giving in. He wasn't parting with his precious old homestead that had been in his family for over a century. Not for an old man's stories, as dear as Old Hannigan was, or the hysteria created by the warnings of one old priest decades ago. "It's all in your head." He kept telling the girls. Until one night a loud, piercing, other-world scream came from the bathroom upstairs. They all rushed up. Mrs. O'Brien was lying on the floor with her hand over her mouth. She had tripped and fell on her way to take a bath.

"I saw someone." She whispered, the colour drained from her face.

"What?" Mr. O'Brien rushed to help her up. "What was it? What did you see, dear?"

"Oh, I'll never forget it. I saw a woman. She was real. She was wearing long, old-fashioned clothes, dripping wet, and she-she was standing right in front of the mirror, combing out her matted hair! The water was flowing in the tub, overflowing onto the floor. I hadn't turned it on. She-she looked so REAL I started to ask her who she was, but then she-she WALKED RIGHT OUT THE WINDOW! SHE JUST FADED AWAY!" Mrs. O'Brien looked at her husband with a new and clear determination.

"Sell this house." She said shakily. "The girls are right. It's haunted. Sell it or you will be vacationing here alone. We want no part of it." Her teacup rattled in its saucer while she tried to sip from the cup Shelley had brought up. Shelley knew her mother had seen the woman from the grate, and the woman on the beach, and the woman in the pictures. And she herself knew those apparitions were all of the same woman,

who , with her baby, had gone to her tragic death too soon in that shipwreck. Like the wails of a banshee, she would forever roam the spot where she had died, crying her anger and her sadness that her
baby couldn't live.

When Mr. O'Brien came downstairs the next morning, his face was grim. "there was someone, a man , a *phantom,* chopping wood out by the woodhorse last night. " he said. "At 3 A.M.!

"How do you know it was a phantom , Dad?" Shelley asked, knowing how skeptical her father was.

"Because I made it my business to go out and see who it was. He looked real, but when I got closer I noticed he wore old-fashioned clothes, and he was dripping wet. I put out my hand, and it went right through him. And then he
...he...*disappeared."* It was strange to see their father so affected.

"We are selling the house." Mr. O'Brien announced finally that evening. "Hardest thing I've ever had to do, but it has to be done. We have to all work together to get it ready."

"Dad!" Shelley screamed one evening. " The pictures keep going back on the wall! When I take them down and go back in the rooms they are all back like no one touched them at all!" She felt sick. She knew that the pictures kept going back because the spirits were inside of them, and didn't want to be moved. Mr. O'Brien shook his head. "I can't explain any of this." He said. "Like Old Dan said, best to get out of here!"

"I can't wait to get out of here!" Sherry said, restlessly organizing her hair berets. "I'm never setting foot in Aspen Falls again! I don't care how scenic it is!"

"I'm never coming here again!" Shelley added.

"When I ask for another ghost story, you have my permission to put me in a retirement home. " said Mrs. O'Brien bitterly. The sign finally went up. The O'Briens went back to the city, two weeks early. The old homestead sold fast. Prime property, in a beautiful pastoral area, not far from the city. A real estate jewel, the real estate agents said. People were falling all over themselves to buy it.

Chapter Twenty-Three

The Ghost Woman Talks

The family was back in the city. But Shelley was restless. In bed, after a long day of settling in, she lay awake for a long time. Almost against her will, she found herself thinking of the woman in the grate, the woman who had frightened her so, and who had manifested herself, her ghost, so many times. Somehow, there was a feeling seeping through her that this spirit was not *meant* to be evil. She thought of the terror and pleading in her eyes when she had gazed at her, so full of bewilderment and fear. A reaching out, to try and show her own terror and helplessness the night she died, the terrible night of the shipwreck. That woman in the grate was one of the passengers who had paraded up the beach from the ghost ship the night of the bonfire. Shelley knew that too.

Those eyes were beautiful eyes, gentle. She had been a gentle woman in life, Shelley felt, and in death, her spirit was not meant to cause fright. A thought formed in Shelley's mind, a thought so unbelievable she wouldn't dare share it with Sherry or her parents, or anyone, not even her friends. Except maybe.....maybe Mrs. Dodd, whose Ouija board Shelley found in the trash.

The Ouija board. Not too many people knew that Mrs. Dodd talked to spirits. Shelley didn't know either, until she found the Ouija board that day, in a pile of trash on Mrs. Dodd's curb. She had been shocked, and intrigued. It was all fun to her then. Mrs. Dodd knew how to communicate with the dead!

Shelley suddenly wished Mrs. Dodd were here now. She would pour out everything that had happened, and find a way for her to communicate with this woman in the grate, and the woman on the beach, and the woman in the pictures. Not to mention the woman in the bathroom! The apparitions were all the same person, she was sure. She sat straight up, rigid, with a rush of adrenalin surging through her. She couldn't believe what was happening to her! She wanted to talk to this woman! This ghost woman from the wreck. She wanted to hear her story. She just couldn't forget those eyes. This sad spirit was trying to make contact; to connect with an earthly presence who would understand, and grant whatever wishes she needed to rest, to cross peacefully over to the other side.

Shelley slept little that night. The next morning, barely eating breakfast, she went out to the portable , prefabricated shed in her parents' backyard. She knew the exact spot where she had hidden it, the Ouija board, after returning from Aspen Falls. In spite of everything that had happened, she had still managed to smuggle it back, in her belongings. For some strange reason, she could not part with it, and had hidden it , underneath the shed. Now she knew why she could not part with it. This Ouija board had work to do.

There was a loose floor board in the shed, underneath which she had placed the Ouija board, pressing it firmly down, and stamping on the floor board to set it in place.

Shelley had marked the loose floor board with a Sharpie marker, so she could find it easily. Her father had come out one day and beaten it back down with the hammer, not noticing the markings. Shelley let out a relieved sigh. If her father had found *that,* after all that had happened in Aspen Falls, there would be hell to pay. She found a crowbar, and eased up the plank.

There lay the Ouija board, wrapped in multiple layers of brown paper, secured with more multiple plastic shopping bags, tied with elastic bands. She withdrew the box, and replaced the loose board, banging it down with the hammer. Then she stopped, holding her breath in nervous anticipation. If someone heard those bangings, her father would be out.

She glanced hurriedly around. She needed something to hold the Ouija board, to disguise it. A blue denim gym bag was dangling from a hook. She placed the board inside it, and slung it over her shoulder. Then she started casually out the yard and down the street. There was a convenience store nearby, and she ordered an ice cream cone. While she ate it, she nonchalantly made her way to the street where Mrs. Dodd lived.

She rang the doorbell. In a few moments Mrs. Dodd opened the door. It occurred to Shelley she did not look at all like a lady who contacted spirits on a Ouija board. Mrs. Dodd looked quite a modern senior lady, in her yellow top and brown leggings, her hair salon-highlighted and trendy gold earrings shimmering from her ears in the crisp morning sunshine.

"Hi, Mrs. Dodd."

"Why, hello Shelley! I haven't seen you in ages! How was your vacation around the bay?"

"It was.....uhh....fine , Mrs. Dodd. But my parents sold the old house, you know."

"*Really?* Oh, that's too bad. But a house that old *is* a lot of upkeep for your parents. Still, it was beautiful, and your father so loved going there. He talked of nothing else. " She looked a little shrewdly at Shelley. Too shrewdly. *She knows* , Shelley thought. *She knows why the house was sold. A woman who talks to spirits on Ouija Boards knows all about old houses, and the ghosts that inhabit them.*

Shelley felt herself going all cold again. Why she didn't know. Was the woman in the grate around, hovering, sensing the vibes from Mrs. Dodd, and the Ouija board, and the chance to make herself known?

"Come on in, Shelley. I just made some tea."

Shelley stepped inside. Her hands were like ice. She had to get this over with.

"Mrs. Dodd, do you believe in ghosts?"

"Ghosts! My goodness, what a question! Of course I don't believe in ghosts! Whatever made you think of such a thing?"

"This." Shelley reached in the gym bag and took out the box. She laid the cumbersome-looking spirit tool on a bench in the hall. Then she quickly undid the wrappings and held it up in front of Mrs. Dodd's startled gaze.

"What in the world....."

"I found it, Mrs. Dodd. In your trash. I know I shouldn't have been looking through your trash, but I was passing by one day and....well....it was just laying there. I couldn't help myself...."

Mrs. Dodd struggled to regain her composure. The secret was out. How embarrassing! Now the whole street, indeed the whole city, would know she talked to a Ouija board; she, who was held in such high esteem for her respectability and community involvement. She glanced sharply at Shelley. She had known this girl all her life. She was smart, and intuitive, and sensible. And something else, something only a like-minded intelligence would decipher. She was honourable. Mrs. Dodd knew her secret was safe with her. But my , it was a shock, to be found out like that. She brushed back suddenly damp wisps of highlighted hair from her brow and went in the kitchen to get cups for tea.

"Whatever in heavens' name are you doing, talking about *ghosts,* a nice girl like you, and on such a beautiful day too.   My *goodness..............*" She placed the teapot and the cups on the table, with jam preserves and muffins, and then she faced the pensive girl.

"Okay. There's something on your mind. What is it?" Her voice was gentle.   Shelley sighed, in inner relief. She knew she could trust this woman.

"Mrs. Dodd, something happened in Aspen Falls, something terrible, which is why Dad sold the house. I don't know if I can even talk about it." But talk about it she did. The words tumbled out. It was good to talk about it to someone who didn't tell her she was imagining things, or to get more sleep, or not to go on the internet.

The sun was going down when Shelley finally got up from the kitchen chair. The teapot had been filled a number of times, but the sandwiches and muffins lay forlornly on plates, waiting to be eaten by two people who lacked any appetite for food of a worldly nature.   Shelley had purged herself of the story, of all that had happened in

Aspen Falls, and her feelings for the ghost woman in the grate.

"You see, Mrs. Dodd, I feel she was trying to make contact with me. I feel she was trying to tell me something."

Mrs. Dodd looked solemn. "Yes, she seemed a very sad woman....a tragic thing. She lost her baby, too. We will see if we can contact her. But you must not be afraid, and you must not tell anyone else about this."

"I promise." said Shelley, a heady mixture of fear and intrigue taking hold of her.

Mrs. Dodd opened the box. She placed the strange-looking board with the mystical patterns and the thing called a planchette on the large, mahagony dining room table. She instructed Shelley to place her fingers, along with hers, on the planchette. Large numerals from 1 to 10, the alphabet, and the words YES and NO formed a gypsy-like semi-circle at the head of the board. Then Mrs. Dodd closed the drapes, switched off all the lights in the house, lit a large candle, and began to talk. She asked a lot of questions.

She asked questions about shipwrecks around Newfoundland's coast over a century ago, and after, and who had died in those shipwrecks. She said she wanted to call forth the spirits of these shipwrecks, and if there were any present, to make contact. She asked questions about the spirits of one shipwreck which had been disturbed by a young man named Hannigan, and who had come back again because Old Mr. Hannigan had broken a pact to keep the curse hidden.

He had brought forth their revenge, Mrs. Dodd went on, and now they had taken up residence in the old O'Brien home in Aspen Falls. Suddenly the planchette, immobile while she talked, now started to move of its own accord around the board. Their fingers were helpless to control its purpose. It moved more rapidly, spelling out letters at random. Mrs. Dodd shook her head in disbelief.

"My goodness! There are a lot of people trying to make contact, from many nationalities. There were a lot of shipwrecks. A lot of people died, horrible deaths. A lot of those ships were lured to shore by false beacons, you know, by cruel livyers who wanted the ships' cargo. They didn't care about the passengers, if they lived or died. The ships crashed on the rocks, and the people perished. Thousands of them. A lot of these same poor souls are here now. They want to talk, but there are just too many of them." The planchette kept moving rapidly, and seemingly desperately around, whizzing from letter to letter, spelling out the names, the flagmasts, and banners of ships from all over North America, and Europe.

"There are just too many." said Mrs. Dodd sadly. "They are not making any sense, and their language is foreign. They are not speaking English. " Suddenly, the planchette stopped, as suddenly as it had started. Mrs. Dodd and Shelley looked at each other.

"I guess we've lost contact." said Mrs. Dodd. "Good thing too, since I'm getting a little freaked out I must confess. I've never experienced *so many* entities trying to make contact all at once like that.

Think I need a coffee." She got up to fill the coffeepot. Shelley kept staring at the planchette . Strangely, she was not at all scared. The feelings of intrigue and fear were now replaced by a new calm, which seemed to envelop her all over. She braced herself. Something was going to happen. They were going to hear from the ghost woman. She just knew it.

The planchette under her fingers started to move again, this time more slowly and deliberately. It stopped before a letter: N. Then another : O. Then R...A...H..

"Mrs. Dodd!" called Shelley. It spelled out N-O-R-A-H....... Norah...a woman's name! Mrs. Dodd sat back down at the table. The smell of freshly percolating coffee was invigorating. She felt now they were about to get some real action, and she could help to put this ghost woman that was so troubling Shelley, finally to rest.

"It could be anybody." She said cautiously. "But I'll see if she has anything to say." She placed her hand, along with Shelley's, on the planchette, and sat up straight. She was as cool as though she were conducting an interview.

"Who are you?" Once again the planchette was a thing alive under their fingers, with a mind and will of its own. It spelled out N-O-R-A-H again, and slowly and purposefully, moved to other letters, spelling out another name: H-A-L-L-E-R-A-N.

"Is your name Norah Halleran?" asked Mrs. Dodd.

"YES." The planchette had moved to the YES caption on top.

"Were you in a shipwreck?"

"YES."

"Where?"

The planchette moved methodically to the appropriate letters.

"Southeast Newfoundland."

"Did you have a baby?"

"YES."

"Did the baby die too?"

"YES."

"Are you happy?"

"NO."

"Did you visit Aspen Falls recently?"

"YES."

"Are you in the old O'Brien home?"

"YES."

At this Shelley became frightened. All of a sudden she wanted to stop. This was a REAL person they were talking to! She felt sick again.

"Mrs. Dodd, I don't think I can do this." She got up from the table.

Mrs. Dodd stayed calm. "It's okay, dear. We have her now. If we don't help her, she will keep coming back. If we can address her concerns, she will be at peace, and won't bother you again." She smiled so serenely at Shelley, with her soulful, pleasant blue eyes, that Shelley felt reassured.

"Ready to go on?" Shelley nodded, took a sip from a strawberry cooler , and sat down again. Mrs. Dodd went on.

"Why did you haunt the O'Brien place?"

"Want gravesite. Want find husband."

"You want gravesite for you? And for your baby?"

"YES. Want find husband."   The planchette was flying now, from letter to letter. It didn't need human fingers to help connect. Norah Halleran herself was driving it, propelling it, in her journey to peace. They could feel the passion and urgency of this young, beautiful woman, whose wishes were coming through, after over a century of   confinement of her soul in a watery grave, not knowing peace.

"Can you tell us why you were on the ship?" The planchette became very erratic. It moved all over the board in a frenzy before it finally came to a stop and started spelling out words, relating the heartbreaking story of Norah Halleran.

"Terrible storm....no lights.....was going to St. John's....meet Richard....

"Is Richard your husband?" Mrs. Dodd had her head tilted, in intense listening, as though she could hear the woman's voice.

"YES. Want gravesite....want find Richard."

"What was your husband's profession?

The plancette moved speedily around. Mrs. Dodd and Shelley felt it was a waste of energy to have their fingers on it. The energy emanating from Norah Halleran was desperate in its quest.

"Storekeeper. Want find Richard. Want my baby and me to sleep beside him, to eternity."

Mrs. Dodd's voice was soothing, assuring.

"We will find Richard. You will be sleeping beside him. We will erect a monument for you and your baby. Your souls will be beside your husband's. In death you will not be divided."

The planchette slowed its speeding motion, moved slowly around one more time, then quietly stopped.

"Thank you." It spelled out.

Mrs. Dodd waited, with her head tilted, a few moments longer. Silence, like that which descended on the old kitchen the night Old Hannigan re-opened the forbidden doors to his memory box, now encompassed the room. But a silence of peace, completion. The planchette lay still. Mrs. Dodd wrapped up the board and looked at Shelley. She was as calm as if she had just completed the minutes of a committee meeting, instead of talking to ghosts.

"Well, I guess our work is almost done for this poor woman. I'll do some research, and find Richard, the husband. When I do, there will be a gravestone erected next to his. She will finally be at peace. " She smiled at the fascinated girl. "It's dark. Do you want to go home or stay here for the night?"

"I'll go home. I'll call Dad to come get me. Thank you, Mrs. Dodd. I feel a lot better now."

"Good. And remember, mum's the word. I'll keep you informed on what I find. But I think you should focus on other things now, enjoy the summer . You're too young to be involved with this kind of thing."

For the next few days, Mrs. Dodd studied geneological circles, parish records, and census data. There were several Richard Hallerans, but finally she found a Richard Halleran who had been a businessman in St. John's in the early

1900's. She found out the location of his gravesite in one of the city's largest cemeteries. The caretaker assisted her in finding the grave. On it, following the details of his birth and death, was inscribed *predeceased by wife Norah and baby daughter Millicent, lost in shipwreck, August 1901.* Mrs. Dodd felt victorious.

After further research, she found information on relatives of Norah Halleran, still living in Newfoundland. Finally, she was pleased to tell Shelley that a headstone for Norah Halleran and her baby had been ordered, to be erected next to her husband Richard, in the same plot. On it was to be inscribed : *Sacred to the memory of Norah Halleran, wife of Richard, and their baby, Millicent, who perished at sea, August, 1901. Rest In Peace. In death, as in life, they are not divided.*

Shelley hugged Mrs. Dodd. She was grateful. The inscription said it so well. She wasn't divided from him in life, nor did she want to be divided from him in death. The woman was at peace, or so she hoped. Shelley felt happy to leave the Ouija board with its owner, and went home satisifed. She was glad to leave it all behind. It was time to try and forget all that happened, and enjoy what was left of the summer.

CHAPTER TWENTY-FOUR

Trying To Forget

"Can't wait for school to start." Shelley was tossing the basketball at a net over the garage carelessly, her heart not really into it. She was bored. They had been back in the city for weeks now, and she had done her best to put the seance with Mrs. Dodd and the Ouija board out of her mind. It was so hard to not tell Sherry or her mother or her friends about that unforgettable evening in Mrs. Dodd's dining room, with the lights out and talking, actually talking to dead people. But none of them would understand. They always looked at her strangely when she mentioned ghosts, like she was unhinged or smoking pot or worse. It was best to keep up the facade of a normal teenager looking forward to a new school year . Sherry picked up the forgotten ball and tossed
it back, bouncing it up and down on the hot, slick pavement of the driveway. She smirked across at her sister.

"Did I hear right? Do I have wax in my ears or what? Did you say you can't wait to go back to SCHOOL? You, who hates books and learning and all things studious?"

Shelley made a face. "Well, I'm sick of summer now. It's too hot. I'm tired of screaming kids at Bowering Park. Tired of crowded swimming pools. Tired of baby-sitting. Tired of riding my bike. Tired of soccer. I'm even tired of yakking on the phone with Vicky Shetfield, listening to her droll on about her latest crush, and I never thought I'd say that. Vicky Shetfield is such a bubble-brain!"

"Are you sure it's not the new guy next door who spurred on this new scholarly interest?" Sherry poised the basketball on her index finger, aiming for another slam-dunk. "He's cute, and he's going to be in our class! I already talked to him."

"Oh, really? Well, that's kinda cool." Shelley answered coyly. "But I
really can't wait to see the new Junior High School they're building all summer, and the new gym. I hear they have an awesome gymnastics class". She fished in a brightly coloured plastic retail bag lying on the grass and waved something at her sister.

"Look!" She flashed her new blue striped gym suit she had just bought at Sears.

"Wow, that's impressive. You really do want to go back. "

Sherry shrugged and thought for a minute. "Well, as long as they have a decent Drama and Glee Club, better than the old school. Old Tessler couldn't sing a note, the Drama coach couldn't act, and no one could read a line of music!" The two girls shared a laugh as their father came in from the backyard, in the act of putting away the whipper-snapper he had been trimming the hedges with. The three of them walked in the house, to help their mother prepare supper, as she drove in the driveway , waving at them after her day in the office .

"Hey, Dad, how's Mr. Hannigan doing?" Sherry was brushing her down-her-back, shiny blonde hair in front of the large, gilt-framed, hallway mirror where she could see herself full-length, and get a good view of her latest pair of stone-washed jeans. She was keeping a wary eye out, since if her mother spied a single hair anywhere near the kitchen and food, she went ballistic, and immediately ordered the girls upstairs to do their primping.

"Hey, Dad, how's Mr. Hannigan doing? "
Shelley echoed her sister.

Mr. O'Brien sighed before he answered.

CHAPTER TWENTY-FIVE

The Curse That Is Old Hannigan

"He doesn't like the nursing home. He wants
to go back to Aspen Falls. But he is too frail now.
His arm keeps getting those awful ugly
red sores, blisters, and the doctors don't know
why. They keep telling him it's a blood infection
to pacify him but he keeps muttering *I should
never have told that story. Let sleeping ghosts lie.*
Everyone there says his mind is going."

"I'd like to go see him." Shelley said. "Poor old
Mr. Hannigan. "

"Me too." said Sherry. "He didn't deserve any
of the stuff that happened to him. He was just a
nice old man." Mr. O'Brien nodded.

"Yes, no matter what, he is still a part of my roots and my youth. I'll never forget old Dan." His face looked a little sad for a second.

"Dad, can we go see him tonight? Please? There won't be much time once school starts." Shelley would also never forget her childhood memories in Aspen Falls, and old Hannigan's beautiful, story-book house, before all the horror happened.

The next evening Mr. O'Brien took the girls to see Mr. Hannigan, at HillView Nursing Home. He was sitting in a large chair in the lounge, a colourful knit throw, a present from Mrs. O'Brien, covering his lap and knees. Shelley sat by him, and linked her arm in his.

"It's good to see you, Mr. Hannigan. We've missed you." The old man smiled a cheerless, toothless smile, but his blue eyes were still lit, and intelligent , and aware. His mind is far from gone, Shelley thought. He's still the same old Mr. Hannigan, and he...he....*knows things.* Suddenly Shelley screamed. Something cold and metallic was linked into her arm. It wasn't Mr. Hannigan's arm at all. It was a hook!

She looked down. Underneath the hanging sleeve of his shirt she could see the upturn of it.

She jumped and put her hand over her mouth to keep from screaming again. She felt like throwing up. She wasn't linked in to his arm at all, but to a hook! Mr. Hannigan's diseased arm was gone! But it didn't seem to faze him at all. He reached out with the hook-hand and picked up a book from the magazine rack next to his chair.

"I'm getting the hang of it." he said, in the same tone he used when he would be starting on one of his stories back in Aspen Falls. "Good play on words eh? Getting the hang of the hook thing. " He grinned a gummy grin, his sunken cheeks more sallow and wrinkled in his collapsed face. "But I should never have told that story. No, I should never have told that story. Let Sleeping Ghosts Lie, that's what I always say. Let them be."

Mr. O'Brien coughed after awhile, and made his excuses.

"Well, Dan, it's great to see you. The girls wanted to see how you were doing. But we have to go now. Have to stop at the Superette."
He walked the girls out through the lounge and corridor to the main door with more speed than usual. In the car , Shelley finally spoke. She felt a slow hysteria rising in her, which had lain dormant the last weeks.

"Dad, his arm is gone! It's just a hook now! Wow, that's just so creepy."

They were driving back in the dark, starry, crispy night. Fall was already in the air, in spite of the heat of the day. Mr. O'Brien was glad the girls couldn't see his shocked expression. The hooked arm had freaked him out too.

"I didn't know he had had the operation, or I would not have brought you girls there. Anyway, forget about it. The doctors did what they had to do, by amputating his arm. Old Dan is being well taken care of. I'll go see him from time to time, but it's too much for you young girls. You got to see him again, and he appreciated it, but I don't want you going there again. It's not a situation for young people. "

They may have taken his arm, but did they get rid of the curse Shelley found herself thinking, and wondered where the words came from all of a sudden.

CHAPTER TWENTY-SIX

Final Revenge

The girls were sitting at supper three weeks later, planning what to buy out of the bonus money their mother had given them after the house sold. It was meant to be a compensation for all they went through in Aspen Falls that summer, and to help them forget. The sight of Mr. Hannigan's hooked arm was the final shocker. They were jubilant over the tickets to a Justin Bieber concert in Toronto, just before school started, and were planning what to wear.

"If you're wearing that pink shift I'm not wearing the same. " Sherry said. "Sometimes it's a real pain being twins. "

"Well, I'm not wearing that sickly green." Shelley came back. "It looks like vomit." Mrs. O'Brien looked shocked and was about to reprimand Shelley, but then gave them an affectionate glance and looked at her husband. It was good to have her old, real, conflicting, spirited daughters back from that other- world realm they had become lost in for awhile , in that terrible time in Aspen Falls. She shivered. She would never forget that nightmarish time, not if she lived to be 200.

Suddenly Shelley dropped her dessert spoon and let out a piercing scream. "Look! Look at this!" She was pointing at The Evening Courier newspaper that was lying forgotten on an extra empty chair at the table.

Four pairs of horror-stricken eyes fixated on the front page, then became glued to it. There was their house! The house that had held such beloved memories, but was now a torture chamber. The article read:

TERROR IN ASPEN FALLS!

HORRIFIC APPARITION CAUSES HOUSE OWNERS TO FLEE

Paranormal True Horror:

The new owners of a quaint, centuries-old saltbox in tourist-paradise Aspen Falls took to the road in terror today, vowing to sue the previous owners, the O'Brien family, who owned the property for generations, for deception of sale ethics: failing to disclose a potentially lethal psychic presence on the property. The terror began in the blackness of dark last night, immediately following deposit of several trunks and crates in the lane, preparatory to moving in.

As the new owners attempted to deposit more heavy articles on the ground and in the yard, the porch lights went out, and they were confronted by a hooked-arm, sloshing wet, headless phantom, dripping blood; a horrific ghostly mass, who growled a deadly warning:

YOU ARE IN THE WAY. NEVER BLOCK A BEATEN PATH. LET SLEEPING GHOSTS LIE.

THE END.

ABOUT THE AUTHOR:

Geraldine Ryan-Lush was born and raised in St. Joseph's, St. Mary's Bay, Newfoundland, surrounded by 100-year-old houses and outbuildings, lamplight and stove song, a setting she recreates so vividly in this novel. In her childhood, berefit of electricity and modern amenities, as was the community at that time, storytelling, especially true tales of the supernatural, was paramount in entertainment. Geraldine peered down through the iron grate in the hallway many nights, and listened covertly to spine-chilling ghost stories she was not supposed to hear! None was more horribly fascinating than that of The Man With No Head, a true, cursed encounter as happened to the family's neighbour and friend, and told and retold throughout Geraldine's young adult life.

After many popular books and stories garnering her international critical acclaim, and a burgeoning interest in the paranormal, she decided to create a work based on, and embodying, this headless spirit who wreaked such havoc on a young man's life. The result is **Hannigan's Hand.** This expanded new edition of the chilling best-seller, **Hannigan's Hand: The Ghost Woman Talks** solves the mystery of the ghost woman in the grate! Geraldine is currently working on a book of terrifyingly true, contemporary ghost stories, as happened in modern St. John's, and environs, slated for 2016 release.

Also by Geraldine Ryan-Lush: (In print)

-Malcolm The Klutz
-Malcolm and the Hamster Lady
-Jeremy Jeckles Hates Freckles
-Hairs On Bears
-Poils Poils Et Repoils
-No Go Potty!
-Miriam Webber Stopped Being Clever
-The Adventures Of Toby Trotter
-Mrs. Woods' Bread
-The Listener
-Mr. Mcguillity's Secret
-The Thing About Amadeus
-A Dark Room Full Of Light
-Katie's Pictures

For Adults:

-The Captain's Lady (Novel)
-Once When I Wasn't Looking (Poetry Collection)

-Awards/Honours

*American Bookseller's Pick Of The Lists
*Merit Magazine Studio Award
*Alcuin Society Design Award
*Awarded major writing grants from Canada
Council for the Arts and NL Arts Council to
further work

*Geraldine Ryan-Lush's books are in numerous
libraries and library systems in U.S. and North
America, as well as U.K. and worldwide. Some are
on the curriculum in schools, and are utilized as
training components for students of children's
literature in several universities. Some are also in
translation.

Contact:

Mulberry Books
27-A Pasadena Crescent
Suite 204
St. John's, NL

Canada A1E4S4

Telephone: 1-709-368-5156.   @GRyanLush
Mobile: 1-709-728-4866
Email: geraldine1942@live.com

****

www.ingramcontent.com/pod-product-compliance
Lightning Source LLC
Chambersburg PA
CBHW060123260626
47160CB00005B/2004